THE
GREAT MAN'S
SECRET

THE
GREAT MAN'S
SECRET

PIETER VAN RAVEN

CHARLES SCRIBNER'S SONS • NEW YORK

Charles Scribner's Sons Books for Young Readers
Macmillan Publishing Company
866 Third Avenue, New York, NY 10022
Collier Macmillan Canada, Inc.

Printed in the United States of America
First Edition   10 9 8 7 6 5 4 3 2 1

Library of Congress Cataloging-in-Publication Data
Van Raven, Pieter, date.
The great man's secret / Pieter van Raven.   p.   cm.
Summary: When fourteen-year-old Jerry, a student reporter, tries to interview elderly Paul Bernard, a truculent legless recluse and the most brilliant novelist in the world, the visit breaks Bernard's case of writer's block and sends him down the long road after memories he has been keeping locked away.
[1. Authorship—Fiction.   2. Physically handicapped—Fiction.]   I. Title.
PZ7.V347Gr   1989   [Fic]—dc19   88-29204   CIP   AC
ISBN 0–684–19041–9

For D. L. D.

THE
GREAT MAN'S
SECRET

1

———— ♦ ————

THE GREAT MAN SAT AND BROODED. IN THE GREAT WHITE house on the cliff he ate and slept and sat and brooded. At evening time, when the blood red sun touched the rim of the ocean, his daughter wheeled him to the deck. Together they watched in silence the day end.

The great man sat and brooded and wrote. Every other year, toward the middle of May, he sent five hundred pages across the country to his publishers. They sent him a check and turned his brooding thoughts into a book.

Prizes and awards came across the country. They were not heeded. One stormy evening a call came from Sweden to offer him the greatest prize of all. No, he would not accept. He would not honor them with his presence. The great man wheeled the chair back to his desk and finished a sentence.

2

DAD SAID THAT WHEN JERRY STARTED HIGH SCHOOL HE should take up a student activity and follow it through. It could be important for getting him into the college he might want to go to.

"I can look after myself now, Jerry. You've been great this last year; you don't have to take your mother's place. I can go back to looking after the house—and you, too."

Jerry knew this was so. That's what Dad had done as long as he could remember, except for the last year, after Mom left to go back to Chicago to find a job and a place to live that was hers.

"You'd better come along with me, Jerry," she'd said. "I can't see that either one of us has any future in this California hick town. Are you sure you want to stay?"

Jerry stayed. He had to finish junior high and he knew Dad would need his help. Mom didn't need him trailing along if she was starting a new life. He stayed and filled in for Dad, who stopped looking after things for a year. Some days he hardly talked.

And the truth was, Jerry knew, he liked it where he was. He was pretty comfortable in the pleasant little house on the pleasant little street in the pleasant little town not far from the ocean and not too far from the mountains. It was where Dad had grown up, and Jerry became part of it, too, as he grew up. Mom was the outsider. "You could put this whole place down in Wrigley Field and still have room to play ball," she used to say.

Jerry understood how it couldn't be his mother's town. After almost fourteen years in Santa Juana she still longed for Chicago. Mom had a professional degree, she kept saying, that she couldn't use. Sometimes, when she was really mad, she said it was a better degree than the one Dad had and maybe he'd like to come to Chicago with her and look after things there while she went to work for a while. Dad always shook his head. "I can't, Amy. This is our home here."

"It certainly is your *father's* home," Mom muttered as she threw her clothes into the big suitcase she had never used and packed up the computer she seldom used. "There's nothing here for me, Jerry, except making the beds and sitting in the sun. I have to have a life of my own. I wasn't meant to spend my life going to junior high soccer games and running the bake table at the school fair . . . I didn't even get a chance to bake the cakes. Dad always has to make his mother's angel food cake. Dad has his ways and I would like to have mine. I have to find out, anyway. Your father and I were probably never meant to be."

Mom sat on the edge of her bed. She buried her face in

her hands and cried. "We both love you, Jerry," she sobbed. "We both love each other in a kind of crazy way, but I am wasting away here. You have to understand that now, so you won't be angry with me afterward. I've spent fourteen years doing nothing, like a tiger in a cage. When you started off to school, I wanted to be a fieldworker, to pick artichokes, anything to feel useful. Dad said I'd put some poor Chicano out of a job. He was right. They don't need a social worker in Santa Juana. They probably don't even know what one is. Last year I took that stupid job in personnel. That wasn't *my* kind of work. I was trained to help people, not select them. I wrote to the director of the social service agency in Chicago where I used to work. I think they'll take me. Maybe I'll change my mind and come back, but now I have to find out some things for myself before it's too late."

Jerry hadn't cried. It seemed to him he had listened to his parents bicker and sometimes shout—Mom, at least—as far back as he could remember. He sat next to her on the bed and felt sad for both of them. They loved him, that was for sure, and put him first. He understood that his mother had to leave. People had a right to do what was important to them. His friends' mothers were busy in the house, but Mom never got used to running a house or shopping or talking to neighbors for a couple of hours or cooking a big supper. After a while Dad started doing these things, and Mom didn't seem to care. She grew up in an apartment, she explained to Jerry, where everyone was busy with things besides running the house.

His mother wiped her eyes. She tried to smile. "You're going to stay, aren't you, Jerry? I could fight it, but I won't. We'll see each other every summer and a week or two in the winter. I'm going to hope that when you finish high school you'll come to college in Chicago."

His mother went away, and Jerry tended house as well as he could until his father began to look after things again.

Jerry spent two summer months in Chicago with Mom in her apartment. She had a friend named Stu who came by to use her computer. When he wasn't doing his research at the university, Stu sat in front of Mom's computer, just sitting there waiting for something to happen. Mom said he was a sociologist. He was writing a book. He took Jerry to Wrigley Field one afternoon and the Art Institute another afternoon. In the evenings when Mom came home from work they ate at lots of different little restaurants and went to lots of movies, some of which Jerry was pretty sure his father wouldn't have let him see. The rest of the time he tried to look after the apartment or went over to the lake for a pick-up baseball game the other kids let him into. Mom was happier than he had ever seen her, and he was happy for her. She fussed over him every minute. Toward the end, Jerry was glad to be going back to Santa Juana to start high school. All her fussing and Stu at the empty computer screen were getting on his nerves.

3

⸻ ◆ ⸻

"WHY, DAD, WHY DIDN'T YOU JUST SAY, 'YES, THANK YOU very much. I am honored,' and take it?"

The great man hunched forward in his chair. "You know why, Lorna. Why do you ask?" he grumbled.

"But the Nobel is no ordinary prize. It's not like the others you don't pay any attention to. The Nobel means you're one of the greatest writers in the world. It comes only once. I know they should have given it to you a long time ago, but they didn't. Now they have. You should accept it, Dad."

The great man straightened up. He always had trouble explaining himself to Lorna—or to anyone else, for that matter. He had given up receiving visitors, even friends who came by unannounced. He had come to believe that his life was private, that what he wrote now was enough of an explanation for anyone who cared to know about him. All he wanted, all he had wanted since the accident, was, as he thought back, to be left alone. He told himself he needed to be alone to brood on humanity and its fate and to write it down.

"We could have gone to Sweden," Lorna was saying, "and had a vacation, Dad. You haven't left the house for, well, I don't know how long. It would do you good, it would do us both good, to have a change of scenery."

"I don't intend to leave, Lorna. You are free to go as you please. Mrs. Bailey can look after me. Haven't you been to Sweden?"

"Several times, and I will go again—by myself—if you accept. I'll stand in for you, Dad, and read them whatever speech or message you want me to deliver."

Now it was becoming difficult. He could no longer stop the conversation where it was. Lorna deserved an explanation. Even though she knew what he was going to say, he had to say it again. He owed her that much and more.

"Ten years ago, I might have said yes. Then again, I might have said no. They owed it to me, and it might have seemed appropriate. Ten years ago, I was the best writer in the country and—"

"Today, Dad," Lorna interrupted, "you may be the best writer in the world. There's a difference."

"Perhaps, but then I was arrogant and vain, and I might have said yes just to prove who I was. But I'm not sure, Lorna, I'm just not sure. Anyway, they didn't give it to me then, and I haven't worried much about it since."

"That's not the point, Dad. You know it's not. We're talking about right now, not something that didn't happen ten or twenty years ago. The Nobel Prize for literature is a recognition of everything you have written. You have an obligation to accept."

The great man listened to his daughter with only half an

ear. "Everything you have written," she had said. And what about what he hadn't written? The best of him lay buried, he knew, where he would, or could, never touch it. He shuddered in his chair. What about that? What was Lorna saying, that he had to accept?

"You are wrong, Lorna. I have no such obligation, not to anyone, not even to you. I have no such obligation to myself. Writers are not ordinary people, Lorna. I am not an ordinary man—I have never tried to be. I don't write for ordinary men or women. They are not interested in me. I am not interested in them. I know what I am and I know what I must do. Those are the facts of my life, not a point of pride. Whether I accept a prize or not, I remain what I am. So, I don't intend to disturb myself."

That was wrong, the great man realized. The explanation was going badly, the way it always went badly when he talked about himself. That was probably why he had given up talking about himself. What he had just said wasn't what he meant to say. He tried to set it straight for Lorna, the only person he loved in the whole world. He tried once more.

"What I mean, Lorna, is that if I accept, I *won't* be the same. I *won't* be what I am, whatever that is. Part of me will belong beyond me. I won't be able to control it. Try to understand that I will be responsible to something else, my fame or whatever you want to call it. I can't let that part of me go. I can't share myself that way. I would have to stop what I am doing and pay attention to something else I don't care about. If I stop what I am doing, I will stop being. You already know that, Lorna."

"I know it, Dad, but it's a hard thing to know."

"Yes," the great man said, and hunched forward in his chair. "It is a very hard thing to know."

4

---♦---

"YOU'RE GOING TO BE LATE," DAD SAID AS JERRY PUSHED his bike down the walk.

Jerry didn't tell him he was already late. It didn't matter to Jerry whether he wrote for the high school paper or not. He wasn't crazy about writing, anyway. The best grade he made on an English paper all last year was a B−. Dad, who taught English at the junior high, tried to take the blame, the way he did when things went wrong for Mom or Jerry. He said it was because of the problems at home. But that wasn't it. Jerry didn't like English much. He wasn't sure he liked school much anymore, either.

Dad had been waiting at home after the first day at high school. He asked how it went, and Jerry said okay. The second thing he asked about was activities. After school was sign-up time for clubs. Jerry said he thought he'd wait for a while, then decide. Dad reminded him that it would be too late. "It's better to start now, son, so that when you're a senior you might get elected to be in charge. That will look good on your record. I don't want to push you, Jerry, but a good college is important. Your mother would agree."

Jerry wasn't sure Mom would agree, but he didn't say so. "I don't know what to choose right now, Dad," he said. "I'm not interested in anything in particular." Which was true. Not sports, not stamps, not science, not acting, not debating, not really any of the things you could go out for. What he did like, they didn't have any club for. That was riding his bike along the back roads, down to the ocean or over to Smithville, when Mom had been around, to bring home the drops in avocado season. He felt free whenever he took off on his bike after school or on Saturdays. He wondered for a moment if, had he stayed home with Mom those times, she might not have left. Jerry didn't think so. His mother told him she had decided a long time ago to leave when Jerry reached high school.

"Why not try the school paper?" Dad asked. "Just for this year. When you're a sophomore you'll know better what to do."

Time slipped away while they were talking and Jerry knew that by now the school paper meeting was bound to be over. When he returned to the high school, Mr. Wilson was packing his briefcase. He sat down at his desk and gave Jerry a questioning look.

"It's too late, isn't it, Mr. Wilson?" Jerry asked. "I mean, too late for the *Scripture*." What a stupid name for a newspaper, the *Santa Juana Scripture*. Dad said the paper had always had that name.

"The meeting is over, if that's what you mean. The editors and the new students and I discussed what we would do this year. To be honest, it won't be much different from last year and the year before. We gave out assignments for the September issue and that was it. You didn't miss much."

Jerry felt relieved. He'd tell Dad he was five minutes too late. He started to leave.

"Just a minute, Jerry," Mr. Wilson called after him. "Do you really want to write for the *Scripture?*"

"I don't know, Mr. Wilson. Dad thinks it's important for me to do some extracurricular stuff. He suggested the paper. While we were deciding, I guess we ran out of time. I'll be here early next year."

Mr. Wilson wouldn't let him go. Jerry could see he wanted to be friendly, probably because he and Dad were both English teachers in the same school system. Maybe it was because Mr. Wilson didn't have a wife and kids of his own.

"What are you most interested in?" Mr. Wilson asked.

Jerry felt himself getting embarrassed. "I don't know," he stammered. "I should have special interests, but I don't. I like sports, but I'm not all that great at them, and I don't want to write about them. Nothing much else, except riding my bike."

"That's what I thought," Mr. Wilson said. "I've seen you on your bike over on the other side of Smithville. What were you doing there? It must be more than ten miles from here."

"When they're picking avocados, they give away the drops. Mom likes avocados. She used to say they were about the only thing she liked about living here." As soon as he said it, Jerry realized that it was none of Mr. Wilson's business. "I'm sorry. I didn't mean it that way. It was just something Mom used to say. She didn't mean anything by it."

"It's all right, Jerry. We all understood Amy wasn't happy

here. I grew up in San Francisco. If I don't get back there for a month or so every year, I feel like I'm going to explode. Santa Juana is a small town. If you grew up in a city, it's pretty hard to take. You're lucky your mother stuck it out as long as she did. She truly loved your dad, didn't she?"

That wasn't anything Jerry wanted to talk about. It wasn't that Mr. Wilson was prying; he was trying to be friendly. Jerry just didn't feel right talking about what went on at home.

"Yes," he said, and headed for the door again.

"Sit down, Jerry, please," Mr. Wilson said. "I have an idea. Will you listen for a minute?"

Jerry shrugged and sat down crosswise in a desk chair. "I have to go to the store on my way home," he explained. "Dad forgot the milk." Right away he wished he hadn't said that, either. It was his day to talk against his parents.

Mr. Wilson didn't seem to notice. "It just occurred to me. You know what we could have for the *Scripture*, Jerry? A traveling correspondent who writes about what's going on outside of town. Someone who keeps track of those things. Someone on a bike. Like you, Jerry."

Jerry was surprised and a little bit interested. So far as he could see, not much more went on outside of town than went on inside. Still, some things were pretty interesting if you paid attention. "Like, what could I look for?" he asked, just to be certain he and Mr. Wilson were talking about the same thing.

"Well, there's that old mission chapel on the road to Silver City. It's the only building left around here from the time the Spanish settled. And I've always been interested in the people who come and go at picking time, those fieldworkers. Where do they stay? Where do they go back to? Things like that." Mr. Wilson paused. He was getting another idea. When he spoke again, he was really excited.

"Look, Jerry, nothing may come of this, but would you like to give it a try? You'd have to do it on Saturday. Do you know the Bernard house?"

Jerry shook his head.

"Down the coast. That big white house way up on the edge of the cliff. I'm not certain the road is paved all the way to the house."

"Oh, that house. It's paved all the way. I went along the county road there once. At the driveway there's a sign that says you shouldn't go up."

"That's Paul Bernard's place. He doesn't allow anyone to come to the house, they say."

"Who's Paul Bernard?" Jerry asked, interested. It sure was a Saturday trip. Even on his new ten-speed bike it could take him two hours to get to the white house. The driveway looked mean. Coming home would take about an hour.

"You don't know?" Mr. Wilson was saying. "Your father never talked about him?"

Jerry wasn't about to let Dad down again. "He probably did," he mumbled, "when I wasn't paying attention. Sometimes Dad talks about things I've never heard of. I'm not any more of a reader than I am a writer."

Mr. Wilson wasn't listening again. He had a funny gleam in his eyes. "It's just possible," he was saying to himself. "He's crazy enough to do it just to spit in everybody's face. It's just possible." Looking at Jerry, he said, "I'm sorry. I was talking to myself. A bad habit unless you're a bachelor. Paul Bernard is the greatest writer alive. He lives in that house with his daughter and a housekeeper. He never leaves, and no one gets in. The two women won't talk about him. After a while, people gave up trying."

"He has no reason to let me in," Jerry pointed out. "What's Mr. Bernard going to see a high school student for?"

"I honestly don't know. He almost certainly won't, but if you're willing to try, why not give it a shot—that is, if your dad says it's okay. Be sure to ask him. If old Bernard did see you, what a coup for us."

"What's a coup, sir?"

"Call me Jake, if you want. All the kids on the paper do. A coup is something important and unexpected—a quick triumph, you might say. You see, Jerry, Paul Bernard has just turned down the Nobel Prize for literature. Said he wasn't interested. He couldn't be bothered to go to Sweden. That's the greatest prize there is. It's worth a lot of money—not that Bernard needs money—and fame. Can you imagine, he said he wasn't interested." Mr. Wilson—Jake—shook his head. "Boy, if that were me . . ." He seemed to forget Jerry was in the room.

"I'll try, Mr. Wilson. I'll give it my best shot." Jerry wondered if that was how reporters talked. He went outside to his bike. Dad would be waiting for him and the milk.

5

———————◆———————

"IT'S NOT GOING WELL, DAD, IS IT?" LORNA ASKED. FOR THE
third time since she had sat down in the enormous room that
served at one end as study for her father and at the other as
reading room for her, the great man had pushed himself
away from the polished slab of mahogany that was his desk.
He rolled his chair to the wall of glass and stared out at the
wallowing, dark ocean. Gulls soared in the wind above the
cliff, their short, sharp cries reaching beyond the glass into
the room.

Paul Bernard doubled his hand into a fist and pounded the
arm of his chair. "No," he responded, "it's not going well."

Lorna hesitated. There was little she could say. Her father
worked at his own pace—a day to brood, a day to write, a
day to correct—over again and over again until he had finished a book. Then he began another. Her father was a machine, she thought, but you could not turn him on or turn

him off. You didn't let anyone interrupt the steady brooding pace of his writing. That was her job now, she realized. Before her, it had been Mrs. Bailey's job. Before Mrs. Bailey, she wasn't sure. She hadn't been here then.

Her job also was to wait, Lorna supposed, wait until whatever it was that slowed the machine down, and now had made it stop, went away. She wasn't sure what to say or do. Since she had come to the big, white house seven years before, the machine had run perfectly. Well, she could wait. She wasn't going anywhere in a hurry.

It wasn't the moment to review her life. She sighed and went to take the leather pouch from the peg by the kitchen door. She strode the twisting mile down to the county road. The mailbox was filled, as usually it was, with letters—complaints, congratulations, advice, requests, reviews. Lorna was familiar with them all. They were her job, too. She pulled them out. She would answer some, discard others, and save others to discuss with Dad when the right moment arrived. She put the occasional letter that was not hers to deal with on the corner of his desk. Sooner or later, he would rip the envelope open, scan its contents, and either scribble a reply at the bottom or on the back or crumple it up and throw it into the square straw basket beside his desk where he threw the yellow pages of the first draft of his manuscripts.

Except for the once-a-year letter from Meredith that usually came about Christmas time, a thick, blue envelope that Dad took tenderly into his two hands. He would turn it over and stare at the back to see where she was writing from this Christmas. Then, carefully, ever so carefully, he'd lean over to place it, unopened, in the basket.

Lorna put the mail in the pouch and headed up the hill. It

was a sullen, damp day. Mrs. Bailey's old Plymouth pulled up alongside. "I don't suppose you want a ride, Lorna?" she said.

Lorna shook her head. "You did the shopping?" she asked.

"Child, I've been doing the shopping every Friday for the last twenty-five years. I missed only once, when my other car gave out. This road will get us all, sooner or later." She laughed. Mrs. Bailey put the Plymouth in gear and rattled out of sight around the turn.

At the house, Lorna walked out to the cliff. From the shore a fog had settled across the water. Below, the heavy, slow waves washed over the rocks. Two sea lions were stretched out asleep on the pebbles just beyond the tide. Lorna shuddered, half with fear, half with happiness. She wanted to hold time still in her hands, to squeeze it tight and never let it go.

As she turned toward the house, Mrs. Bailey was rolling Dad onto the deck. "He had to come out," she shouted. "He wouldn't even let me put the frozen food in the freezer. He had to come out this minute. He wants to know if the sea lions are there," she said.

Dad looked thoughtful while Jerry told him about his talk with Mr. Wilson. "It's a long ride, son. And almost certainly for nothing."

"I've been up to their mailbox, up to where the sign says no trespassing. It's about an hour and a half," Jerry said proudly.

He could see that his father's thoughts, just like Mr. Wilson's, were far away. Jerry put his head over his plate of spaghetti and ate.

"Paul Bernard," his father said softly. "Paul Bernard. I

don't recollect that anyone has actually seen him since he moved there. He's supposed to be paralyzed or something. Well, Jerry, you have your work cut out for you. I wonder what made Jake think you had a story there."

"I don't know," Jerry replied. "He said something like, 'Maybe, just maybe.' I can at least do a color story on what it's like up there close to the house. For the next issue, maybe I could write an article on the Chicanos. Will you help me, Dad?"

"Of course I will, but you'll have to write it first, and then we'll talk about it and correct it if it needs correction."

His father stopped talking. He got up from his chair and went into his study. He returned with a book in his hand. He looked inside. "This is one of his early novels. It's the only book I have by Bernard. He's too difficult for me. He's worse than Hardy to read."

Jerry took the book. *The Land Beyond*, it was called. He read the first lines of the first page. Dad was right. It *was* hard to read. But he wasn't much of a reader. One of the few things Mom and Dad agreed on was that their only child was a dreamer, and that was fine with them.

"He'll be all right, Ted," Mom used to say when Dad wanted to push him gently into doing something. "He's not like either one of us, that's all. He finds things out for himself. He'll be all right."

Jerry thought he'd better find out one thing for himself if he was going up to the cliffs tomorrow. "Tell me about Mr. Bernard, Dad. I ought to know something just in case he lets me in."

"There's nothing I can tell you, Jerry; nothing much anyone else can tell you, either. He's a writer. People who read what he writes say he's the best writer there is."

"In the whole world?" Jerry asked, astonished.

"In the whole world, yes. Early this week they wanted to give Paul Bernard the Nobel Prize for literature. He turned them down, and they don't know what to do. They probably won't give the prize this year."

"Why did he say no?"

"For the same reason he says no to every other prize and honor they want to give him, I guess. I don't think I'd turn down three hundred thousand dollars. How about you, Jerry?"

"Gee, I don't know, Dad. If he doesn't want it, I guess he doesn't want it. He just wants to be left alone, it looks like."

"But you're going up to see?" his father asked with a smile.

"Aw, come on, Dad. He's not going to see me. I like to ride my bike. You know that's the reason. If I thought he'd let me in, I wouldn't go near the place."

6

IT WAS A GOOD DAY FOR RIDING. A THICK HAZE COVERED the sun. An ocean chill was in the air. Jerry swung through Smithville toward the intersection where he could pick up the county road that climbed toward the cliffs. That road was graded into easy curves as it went into the hills. Jerry knew he would not have to shift all the way down until he came to the Bernards' private drive.

He pulled up at the big mailbox. BERNARD it said in plain black letters. Across the drive, another sign with plain black letters told him NO TRESPASSING. Jerry decided it wasn't really trespassing if he stayed on the road. If Mr. Bernard didn't want anyone to come up to his house, maybe he shouldn't have built a road. If he was really serious about it, he should have put a chain across the entrance, the way people did for their beach houses. He slipped into the lowest gear and began pedaling up the narrow drive.

No curving grades here. The bends were sharp and flat, and the straight sections went up at an awful angle. Mr. Bernard didn't need a sign. No one would go up that road to the big, white house unless he had to. Jerry swung off his bike for good and pushed it along ahead of him.

At the top, the drive widened into a parking area in back of the house. A beat-up old Plymouth stood in front of the closed garage doors. At one side there was some sort of a courtyard with a couple of garbage cans; some dishtowels were hanging from a clothesline. Everything looked empty.

Jerry knocked at the back door. He waited. There was no response. He knocked again, harder and longer this time. The sound of steps came near. The door opened. A friendly-looking woman with gray hair stood in the doorway. "Didn't you see the sign?" she asked, not in an angry voice.

"Yes, ma'am, I saw it." Dad had said, "Whatever happens, be polite. Most likely, they'll ask you to get on your bike and leave."

"You saw it and you didn't pay any attention." The woman laughed. "Just like my two boys when they were growing up. Signs weren't for them; they were for somebody else. What are you selling? Raffle tickets, magazine subscriptions, charity tickets? Whatever it is, I'll take something. No one ought to come up that hill and go away empty-handed. Wait here, I'll fetch my purse."

"No, ma'am. I mean, no tickets, ma'am. I want to talk to Mr. Bernard, please." Before the woman could cut him off, Jerry got the rest of it out. "I'm a reporter for the *Santa Juana Scripture*; that's our high school paper. They didn't have anything for me to do in town, so they gave me the county to cover. That's because I like to ride my bike. My English teacher—I mean, he'll be my teacher next term—

thought maybe I could have a short interview with Mr. Bernard."

"Mr. Bernard doesn't give interviews, son," the woman said in a kind voice. "Even if you came all the way from China, not just from Santa Juana, he wouldn't give you an interview."

"That's what Mr. Wilson and my dad both said. It was worth a chance, anyway. Could I look over the cliff, ma'am, while I'm here? This part of the coast is hard to get to. I'd like to see what it's like, if that's all right with Mr. Bernard."

"He won't mind. He won't even know you're here. You go have a long look. The view isn't so good today. Lorna said the sea lions were down there. You might see them."

Jerry leaned his bike against the garage. He went around the corner of the house toward the edge of the cliff. It was a huge house, just how big you couldn't see from the back. Mr. Bernard had to be rich to live in a house like that with so much land. He reached the edge. The fog was beginning to lift, as it usually did for a couple of hours in the afternoon. Just in front of the fog line a cabin cruiser was making its way up the coast. The sea lions were still there. While he watched, one of them flopped over and yawned. Jerry was pleased. What a neat place, he thought. A bike wouldn't do you much good up here. You'd have to leave it down by the mailbox.

"It's beautiful, isn't it?" a voice almost at his elbow said.

Jerry was startled. He turned quickly to see a tall, blond woman looking at the ocean, too. She was a little older than his mother, maybe not as pretty, but nice looking in a different way.

"Yes," he managed to reply. "The woman at the back said I could have a look before I left."

"Are the sea lions still down there?" the woman asked. "They go away toward evening. I don't know why."

"I think they like to eat before dark," Jerry said. "That's what my dad told me when we went to Point Lobos. They have to eat an awful lot to stay alive."

"I'm Lorna Bernard," the woman said. She offered him her hand.

Jerry took it and squeezed and then shook, the way Dad told him to do. "I'm Jerry Huffaker. I came up to talk to Mr. Paul Bernard. The woman at the back said he doesn't give interviews."

"That was Mrs. Bailey. She doesn't like to chase people away. Neither do I. We think my father should see other people every once in a while. But he won't. What paper are you from, Jerry?"

"It's only the high school paper in Santa Juana. It's called the *Scripture*. That's a dumb name for a paper, the kids say."

"And they sent you all the way up here to talk to Dad. They must have known he was a very private person."

"They told me that. They wouldn't have suggested it, except that they know I like to ride my bike. Anyway, I'm glad I came even if I didn't see your father. I wouldn't have known what to say. I don't know anything about him except that he didn't take a famous prize."

"The Nobel Prize for literature, Jerry, that's what he turned down. That tells you something about him you need to know. Mrs. Bailey and I are very upset."

"Well, I'll be getting back down the hill," Jerry said. "Thank you and Mrs. Bailey for letting me have a look."

Lorna Bernard stared at him a funny way. She was chewing on her lower lip. "Wait a minute," she told him. "You came a long way up a nasty hill. Dad will have to say no for himself. I won't do it for him this time."

Lorna ran up the path to the deck. She pulled the sliding door open. On his side of the room, his cave, as they called it, Bernard had pushed himself away from his desk again. He was sitting there like an old bear, Lorna thought, waiting for someone to come by to snap at.

"There's a boy outside, a nice kid who wants to interview you," Lorna announced. "You have to see him."

"Lorna, please," her father grumbled. "Let's not go into that again. I'm having enough troubles right now. I don't want to talk to a child."

"You have to, because I'm not going to chase him away for you. He's quite remarkable. Imagine, Dad, he had never heard of you until yesterday. All he knows is that you turned down some kind of a prize he has never heard of, either. You're a nobody to him and he's a nobody to you. That makes you even, Dad."

The great man pondered what his daughter had said. He had felt like a nobody for the past week, ever since that call from Stockholm. He couldn't remember when he had ever let a week slip away from him without writing a single worthwhile sentence. He sighed. "I'll do it, Lorna. Ask him in. And don't go away. After ten minutes, get him out."

Lorna smiled. She strode out the open door. Jerry was peering down at the pebbled beach. "Come on in, Jerry. Dad would like to talk to you."

Jerry approached her slowly. "The sea lions," he told her, wonder in his voice, "they just flopped out into the water. One of them nudged the other with his nose to wake him up—maybe it was a her—and they went into the water together. I've never seen that before."

7

THE GREAT MAN WHEELED HIMSELF OVER TO LORNA'S CAVE, the furnished half of the room. Not that he had any need for furniture. All he used was his chair and a bed. From one to the other and back again: that was the routine of his life. On nights when he wasn't tired, he set his chair back and sat in front of the glass wall, looking at the lights of the fishing boats until he fell asleep.

He waited now in Lorna's end of the cave, expectant and fearful, gazing at the only one of all of Lorna's drawings that she would allow to be hung. It was of himself brooding in his chair near the cliff, his countenance fixed on the horizon. How long had it been since he had spoken to anyone face to face, except for Mrs. Bailey and Lorna? What did one say to a teenager? Lorna was the only child he had ever known, and he never knew the all of her. Thoughts of Lorna led to thoughts of her mother, the rich and elegant Meredith, the woman he should not have married. Her leaving him still hurt. He turned the memories away. All that was a long time ago, he told himself.

He was somehow surprised that it was a nice-looking kid who trailed Lorna across the room, a nice, serious-looking kid. What had he been expecting? he asked himself. The boy was worried, Paul Bernard could see. The room was bound to startle him. He straightened up as Lorna and the kid approached. He thrust out his hand. "I'm Paul Bernard. I am delighted Lorna asked you in. I sit here and I sometimes forget there are people beyond this room and beyond the house. I am very pleased to have you visit us."

The kid took his hand. He finished looking around the room before he faced the great man directly. "It's a big room, all right. It must be almost the whole first floor."

"It is," Lorna told him. "There are a couple of little rooms and the kitchen out back and that's all."

"Upstairs is the same?" Jerry asked. These weren't the questions he should be asking, but he had never seen a house like this. He was more than just curious, he realized; he *had* to know.

"Big bedrooms mostly, and a studio for me and a study for Dad next to his bedroom. He never uses it."

"There's an elevator, in case you're wondering, over there in back of my desk," Bernard said.

Jerry hadn't been wondering, but he knew he probably would have later. Imagine having your own elevator just to get up to the second floor!

"Lorna didn't give me your name," Bernard told him.

"Oh, I'm sorry." Jerry blushed. It was going to be another bad day. "I'm Jerry, Jerry Huffaker. I'm from Santa Juana. I go to high school there."

"Are you a Gerald Jerry?" Bernard asked.

"No, sir."

"A Jerome Jerry?"

"No, sir. My full name is Jeremiah. Nobody calls me that anymore. My mother used to when she was upset."

"Why did she do that, do you think?"

"I don't know, sir. Maybe she had a better idea of who I was if she called me Jeremiah. Jerry doesn't mean much."

Bernard smiled slightly at his daughter. "Shall I tell him, Lorna? Do you know what, Jerry? The second novel I wrote was called *The Discontented*, and it was about a man in the Bible. His name was Jeremiah, too. Have you ever heard of him?"

Jerry hadn't. Mom and Dad didn't belong to any regular church. For a year or two he went to a Sunday School a couple of blocks in back of his house. Mostly they sang songs and listened to stories. He remembered now that they gave out Bible cards, pictures of Moses and Jesus and Mary. He was pretty certain there wasn't a Jeremiah among them. He wouldn't have forgotten that. Anyway, Mom hadn't named him after someone in the Bible. She was the one who wanted him to be a Jeremiah. He had a feeling Dad would have liked him to be an Edward Junior.

"No," he answered, rousing himself from his thoughts. From now on, he had better attend to what Mr. Bernard was saying. Dad and Mr. Wilson would think talking to Mr. Bernard was awfully important. They would want an accounting of every word.

"I'll give you a copy if we have any around. Do we, Lorna?"

"I don't think so, Dad. You've never been very careful about keeping copies of your books. I guess Meredith wasn't, either."

"Oh, yes. Indeed she was. She always kept five or six copies. Maybe she took them with her or maybe I gave them away when I was moving out here. Or maybe they were lost along the way, who knows?"

Paul Bernard noticed Jerry's puzzlement. "Family business, Jerry. Meredith is Lorna's mother. She's been gone a long time. We're not sure where she is now."

"That's not fair, Dad. I know perfectly well where she is. You would, too, if you would read her letters. I'm sorry, Jerry. How did Dad and I get started on this old argument?"

"The book about Jeremiah," Jerry said. "I'd probably have trouble with it. I'm not much of a reader. Dad showed me a book of yours. I tried to read it, but I wasn't ready for it." He kept saying the wrong things, yesterday with Mr. Wilson and today with Mr. Bernard. He was here to interview the man, not insult him. "But Dad read it," he went on. "He said it was like Hardy, whoever he is."

"That's high praise." Paul Bernard laughed. "Thomas Hardy and I. He was a very great writer, Jerry, who didn't like the way the world worked. Neither do I. We are probably the last of the dinosaurs."

"Dad," Lorna objected again. "I don't think Jerry can write a story about your being a dinosaur, whatever you mean by that."

The great man laughed again. This time it didn't sound like a very happy laugh. Things didn't seem to be going well. Jerry began to understand why Mr. Bernard kept to himself. He was a little weird.

Paul Bernard turned to him. "We had better do what Lorna says for a while: no more dinosaur talk. What I meant was that I write seriously. My books are sometimes hard to read. People who read what I write have to think. That is something of a problem these days."

"But you just won a prize, a big one," Jerry answered.

"That was for staying alive sixty-five years. All right, Lorna. I promise. No more talk like that. I'll mind my manners. What's your newspaper called, Jerry-Jeremiah?"

Jerry didn't want to answer. As soon as he told Mr. Bernard the paper was called the *Scripture*, he would start talking again in ways Jerry didn't understand. He had to answer. "It's the *Scripture*, sir," he muttered.

"Jerry, what's this 'sir' business? I'm a Paul, not a 'sir,' and you're a Jerry, unless I want to call you a Jeremiah, which I gather is all right, too. If you and I are going to get along, you call me Paul. Agreed?"

"Yes, sir. I mean, Paul."

"Good. Now, tell me what you are supposed to be doing for the *Scripture*. That's kind of a dumb name for a paper, wouldn't you say, Jerry?"

Jerry smiled for the first time. "That's what all the kids say. I mean, high school isn't Sunday school."

"But it's an old name, too, I bet. Santa Juana is an old town, they tell me. We mustn't forget traditions. That's all we have to hold us together these days."

"Dad!" Lorna interrupted. She was curled up on a big leather sofa, Jerry noticed. She looked pretty happy, too, not worried the way she had been outside. He wondered if she was secretly laughing at him. "Do you know what he's saying, Jerry?" she asked.

"I think so. If they changed it to the *Santa Juana News* or something like that, the kids wouldn't pay much attention. This way we sort of have to put up with it, even though we joke about it and sometimes wonder how it ever got such a dumb name."

Paul Bernard put his big gray head back and roared with

laughter. "There you are, Lorna. You ask a question, you get an answer. Good for you, Jerry. Now, what are we supposed to be talking about?"

Lorna looked at her watch. Jerry had already used up over twenty minutes. Ten minutes, her father had said, ten minutes and get the kid out of here. It was too bad Dad had used up all the time fooling around.

"Dad, it's about twenty minutes," she said.

The great man looked at her blankly. "Twenty minutes? What are you talking about, Lorna? Twenty minutes to what?"

"Twenty minutes. Two times ten, Dad. That's twenty minutes."

"Oh, *that* twenty minutes. It's time for my afternoon cocoa, Jerry. Yes, thank you, Lorna. Would you like some cocoa, Jerry? Of course you would. Tell Mrs. Bailey to make a potful, Lorna. Jerry and I are going to have a long talk."

8

"HONESTLY, DAD, ALL THAT TALK MRS. BAILEY AND I HAVE put up with about not letting anyone bother you, and you sat there talking to that boy about absolutely nothing until it was almost too late for him to make his way home. You should be ashamed of yourself. I suppose I should have called his father, but I had a feeling Jerry wouldn't have wanted me to."

The great man sat hunched over in his chair. He heard Lorna, but he didn't pay very much attention. He spoke, half to himself. "He was a nice kid. I've forgotten what kids are like. He was so honest with me. He didn't care who I was."

"He *was* nice," Lorna agreed. "You should have seen him watch the sea lions waddle into the water together, the way they do sometimes, like a fat married couple setting off for church. You can see that Jerry studies things."

"He's a writer," Paul Bernard decided.

"You heard him, Dad. He said he didn't read much and he didn't like writing. Why do you say he's a writer? Is that what you wanted me to be, Dad, or did you just want a boy instead of a girl? Are you trying to get rid of me, Dad?" she teased.

Bernard raised his head. "I lost you once, Lorna. I won't let it happen again. Whatever love is, it came to me with you. That's why I'll never forgive your mother for carrying you off."

"You could have come after me. You could have sent lawyers after me."

"I was learning to be an invalid. I discovered you can't chase people when you're in a wheelchair, nor will they let you bring up a child when you're in a wheelchair. Meredith knew that."

"Let's not fight the war again, Dad. It's over. I am here. You are here. And she's there."

"Those years," the great man complained. "Those years without my child. Those are lost years. I won't get them back. Your mother didn't want you."

"You're being foolish, Dad. You didn't lose anything. You gained something. Those are the years that made you rich and famous. You wrote it all out, Dad, one way or another. There was no one around to disturb you. Look at it this way—Mother and I got you the Nobel Prize." She laughed at the great man as he began to protest. "Don't talk back. I'm going to help Mrs. Bailey fix our supper."

Paul Bernard wheeled his chair to the glass. No sunset this evening. The fog was rolling all the way to the shore. Soon it would rise up the cliff and envelop the house in a gray, damp blanket. He was alone again. Not alone to brood, he realized, as he generally did in the last hours of the day before the darkness took over. Tonight was different; that much he understood. The friendly little kid from the high school had left something behind that he knew he would have to deal with. What it was, he was not yet certain. It would come to him. He had learned to wait for things to come to him so he could ponder and turn them into books.

Had he himself once been like this fresh-looking kid with a few summer freckles left on the bridge of his nose? Jerry had spoken of his father once or twice, he recalled, with such obvious affection that Bernard was surprised. Did kids still love their parents? No mention of his mother. Gone, he supposed. Bernard hadn't asked. Anger began to surge within him again. He held it back. Lorna was right. The war was over. Meredith was gone. She had been gone for thirty years. Lorna was right. That was too long ago to remember, too long ago to fight. Still, he wondered where Jerry's mother was. He would find out next Saturday.

"I was worried about you, son," Dad said when Jerry burst into the kitchen, out of breath. "It's dark outside, and you don't have any lights on your bike."

"I'm sorry, Dad. I won't be late again. Anyway, I'm going to put a reflector strip on the back fender. Maybe I'll put a couple of strips on my old jacket and wear it if there's a chance I'll be out late."

His father looked at Jerry. "Do you plan on being out late a lot, Jerry?"

"No, but maybe there will be something going on up at the high school I'll want to go to. It's not a bad idea, you know."

"I know. Sit down and tell me what you did while I put the spaghetti in. Do you want garlic bread?"

"Plain is all right. You'll never guess, Dad. I was up at the Bernards'."

"You were at the Bernards' all this time? That's really something. Jake won't believe it."

Jerry didn't answer. He set two places at the kitchen table. They were out of paper napkins. He wrote them down on the memory board. Milk for himself and a glass of red wine for Dad. What would he tell Mr. Wilson? Mr. Bernard hadn't said anything important about himself or what he was doing. He kept teasing Lorna about things Jerry didn't know about. With Jerry he was half teasing, half serious. It was sort of confusing. The interview had never got started. Well, he had a week to plan what he would say next Saturday.

Dad was talking to him. "What a story, Jerry! Don't you think Jake is going to be excited? Paul Bernard is famous for not talking to anyone at all."

"Not since she's been living there, his daughter said, and probably before that, too. It wasn't an interview, Dad. We just sat and talked, the three of us. Mostly I listened and answered their questions. It was almost like they were interviewing me."

"He's lonely, I suppose, up there on the cliff. It must be hard for his daughter, too. Can he get around?"

"Only in his chair. I don't think he has any legs, Dad. He keeps a blanket over his lap. And he has an elevator. It's at the back of the big room, somewhere behind his desk. It goes up to his bedroom, he said."

His father was taking out the spaghetti. He filled two bowls, spooned sauce over the top, and put the bowls on the place mats. He put the breadboard between them.

"I've heard he's paralyzed. Whatever it is, it's too bad. It probably explains a lot about how he writes."

"I'm going back next Saturday," Jerry said. "Lorna said I should eat lunch there. I'll get my interview then. You know, Dad, I have a feeling he just wanted to talk to someone different, someone maybe who's not after him for something."

His father thought about what Jerry had said. There were times during the past year when he would have given anything for a friend to listen to his grief. Amy was the person he told his problems to—before she became the problem. He wondered if Paul Bernard had chosen (well, not chosen, since it was Jerry who had made his way up to Bernard's house—latched on to, maybe, was better) his fourteen-year-old son as a confidant.

"Perhaps you should wait to tell Jake. Could you say that Paul Bernard promised you the interview next week? After that, you'll have something to write about."

Jerry sucked in the last strand of spaghetti. He was still hungry. Maybe Dad would take him out to the Dairy Queen, since it was Saturday night. "That's a good idea, Dad. I sure don't have anything to write about now. Hey, Dad, do you suppose we could go out for an ice cream? We haven't been to the Dairy Queen for quite a while."

"You're right, Jerry. It has been a while, and tonight we have something to celebrate. I'll get my keys."

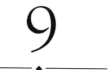

9

PAUL BERNARD, IT SEEMED, HAD WRITTEN HIMSELF NOTES on his yellow paper. Astonished at his discovery, he pored over what he had written on half a dozen sheets of paper and shoved to one side of his desk. Sentences, bits of sentences, a couple of short paragraphs, one or two words here and there, all underlined twice. Each fragment was separated by a strong, black line from one side of the page to the other.

When had he done this? he puzzled. Yesterday? The day before? What was the point of these stray comments? Since he had begun writing, he had never worked from notes. When he finished writing one day, he marked what he wanted to change or cut or expand; the next day, he rewrote. That section finished, he brooded and planned on what was to follow. No notes, no reminders. Those were for other writers. If he couldn't keep what he was doing or going to do in his head, it probably wasn't worth doing. His pride as a writer rested in the *how* of his art, not the *what*. Everyone had something to write about, he had once told Lorna, but not many ever got around to it. It was probably just as well.

How to explain, then, these scribbles spread out in front of him? Clearly they were from the forbidden land, the strange and beautiful and, at the end, frightening territory of his youth and early manhood, that part of his life that he had posted with a thousand NO TRESPASSING signs. Not that it was sacred; it was forbidden. When he was young and wild in love with his precious Meredith, he had begun, only just begun, to share those years with her. The accident put an end to all that, as it had put an end to Meredith and their marriage. Since the accident, he had refused to go back to those years.

But now, here in front of him, were words, not words that he had chosen, but words that had made their way up from his memory, had slipped past the signs when he wasn't paying attention and put themselves, you might say, on paper.

It was the kid, of course. He had recognized himself as soon as Jerry came into Lorna's cave Saturday afternoon. There was that picture his mother had the photographer take when Paul was twelve or so, hair brushed back, unsmiling and intent, his hands folded awkwardly. There he was in his first long pants suit, framed in silver, on the middle of his mother's bureau. Later the picture would be moved to the seaman's chest Dad kept beside his own bed. Now it lay, face down, in the bottom drawer of the three-drawer file cabinet Lorna had bought for him to hold those things he was not brave enough to discard. There lay the boy Paul Bernard, and if you looked closely you would find a reasonable resemblance to another boy, serious, freckled, and thoughtful, the boy who had pushed his bike past the sign up a twisting mile of road to bang on the door of the great man's past.

That was what the scribbles were about. He couldn't work his way around them. There was no point now in crumpling them up and dropping them in the square straw basket. That wouldn't be the end of them. First, there had been that wretched call from Stockholm to tell him what he already knew and didn't want to know. That he was in fact, at least in *their* fact, a great man. Second, there was that forbidden visit past the forbidding sign by a kid on his bike. It was too much for an old cripple to fight against.

"Lorna," he shouted.

"I'm right here, Dad," she answered from across the room. "You don't have to shout."

"Are the sea lions out today?"

"I'll have a look. They should be down there. It's a nice day to sun yourself."

She returned in a few minutes. "They're both down there, sound asleep and snoring in each other's ears."

"I'll go see them. It's been a long time. Where did you put my crutches?"

"Dad, you haven't used them since I don't know when. Let me push you."

"I want my crutches and those fake legs. Where did you put them?"

"You gave up on those legs and crutches years ago, Dad. You said you could get around better in your chair."

That was true, the great man realized. Once they had made him, they said, the finest fake legs money could buy; but who had time to strap them on and take them off? Even Mrs. Bailey complained at times. And he still had to use those crutches. It took time from his writing and, in the end, he settled back into his chair and got on with his life, which was writing books. Well, he wasn't writing now while he was waiting for things to come to him; he might as well try the legs again.

"That may be, Lorna," he said, "but that was yesterday, and today is today. I want to stand up and look down at the sea lions."

"Just the way Jerry did, eh, Dad? You're going out there with him on Saturday, aren't you? May I call the doctor first?"

"Go ahead. Tell him I'll do it no matter what he says."

Lorna went into the kitchen. "He wants out of his chair, Mrs. Bailey. He has the idea he must have a look at the sea lions again. You'll have to help me."

Mrs. Bailey sighed. "We can probably do it together. Those steel things are an awful bother. There were days long before you came when I wanted to tell him to get himself a full-time nurse, that I was just a housekeeper. We had to go out to the cliff every day, rain or shine. You would have thought those sea lions were dinosaurs or something he had to keep track of."

"I remember," Lorna agreed. "Perhaps that's why I never came to visit him often. I couldn't get used to his fake legs, as he calls them."

"He never got used to them, either," Mrs. Bailey went on. "They hurt. After a while, he gave up and went back to his chair. It certainly made my life easier."

Lorna dialed Dr. Koben's number in San Francisco. Once a year Dr. Koben drove down to the big white house to check up on his most celebrated patient. Once a year he examined Bernard and had lunch and went away with his samples. As far as he could see, Dr. Koben told Bernard and Lorna and Mrs. Bailey, everything was just fine.

Lorna explained her father's sudden decision to leave his chair. Was he strong enough now? she asked.

"Paul has the constitution of an ox, Lorna. It will be hard for him at first. He didn't like them, and he hasn't forced himself to use them for a long time. He'll hurt, he knows that, and it will be awkward. You'll have to help him along. If he falls, well, he's fallen lots of times and survived. He won't listen to me anyway. What do you think he's taken into his head?"

Lorna didn't see any point in telling Dr. Koben that her father was intent on showing off to a fourteen-year-old. "He wants to look at the sea lions," she explained.

"Good idea," Dr. Koben said cheerfully. "He needs an outside interest. Give him my best. I'll be down next April."

Jerry managed to avoid Mr. Wilson on Monday and Tuesday. On Wednesday, he was trapped in the cafeteria.

"How was your bike ride up to the cliffs, Jerry?" Mr. Wilson asked. "Saturday wasn't much of a day, was it? I wondered whether you'd try it or not."

"It was good weather for riding," Jerry said. "I don't mind sunny days, but it's easier to go on a bike when it's cloudy."

"You went up to Bernard's house?"

Jerry nodded.

"And?"

"Well, I'm going back on Saturday," Jerry answered honestly.

"Do you mean old Bernard is actually going to see you?"

Jerry didn't like Mr. Wilson calling him "old Bernard." He wasn't so old. Half the time last Saturday he acted like a kid. "I hope so," he told Mr. Wilson. That was an honest answer, too. He tried to shift Mr. Wilson's attention. "It's a great view from up there. And you can look down to the beach and watch a couple of sea lions. Mr. Bernard's daughter said they spent most of their time down there."

"His daughter? You talked to his daughter? Lorna Bernard? I've heard she's not married."

Jerry didn't know whether that was so or not. He nodded, to be on the safe side. He gathered up his tray. "I have to go to class now, Mr. Wilson." That wasn't actually true.

"Jake, remember? Call me Jake. Good luck on Saturday. Boy, would that be a coup."

He was going to have trouble with Jake, Jerry suspected, if he ever had a real interview with Mr. Bernard. It had been his idea to start with. Jerry had a funny feeling that Jake was more interested in Mr. Bernard as a famous person than in Mr. Bernard himself. He'd have to talk it over with Dad. Right now it didn't look to him as though he would ever have a real interview, whatever that was, with Mr. Bernard. That didn't seem to be Mr. Bernard's way.

10

THE SUN WAS OUT SATURDAY. BY THE TIME JERRY REACHED
the Bernard house, his shirt was wet. His sunbleached hair
was plastered over his forehead. He noticed the inside door
to the house was open. He tapped on the aluminum door.

Lorna stuck her head out the door. "Come on in, Jerry.
Excuse me, I'm cooking today. Mrs. Bailey bought some
sodas. They're in the refrigerator over there. Help yourself."

Jerry got out a root beer. He looked around the kitchen. It
seemed to occupy almost half of the back part of the house.
Beyond where Lorna was working at the counter and the
stove was a kind of dining area. He counted four places.

"Sit down, Jerry. I almost called you earlier to see if you
wanted me to come and give you a ride. I decided getting
here was part of your business, not ours. Was I right?"

"Yes, ma'am," Jerry said. He sat down at the heavy
wooden table. It looked like oak, an expensive table, you
could tell.

"Do you want me to be a Lorna or a ma'am? Last Saturday I was both, I seem to remember."

"'Lorna' is what I should say," Jerry replied. "The trouble is I always feel a little strange in new situations."

"You were here last Saturday, so it can't be too strange. And I heard Dad ask you to call him Paul. Mrs. Bailey is a Rose, but you'd better stick with 'Mrs. Bailey.' That's what Dad and I call her."

"That's fine with me, except for your father. Sometimes it doesn't feel right to call people by their first names." Jerry knew that Mr. Wilson would never be a Jake to him, no matter how many times he had to call him that.

"Dad and I shouldn't force ourselves on you, Jerry," Lorna said. "You do whatever is natural to you."

"I sort of like 'Mr. Bernard' right now. I think I know what it means a little bit. 'Paul' is something different."

Dad was always right when it came to sizing up people, Lorna thought. Jerry was a sharp kid. He knew where he stood. "What do you call your mother?" she asked. She had a thing about what "Mom" meant, and "Mama," which was something else, and "Mummy" (ugh!), and even "Mother," which lots of girls at her college used. She and Dad argued about it. Dad said it made a difference only to the child; a mother was pretty much a mother no matter what you called her.

Jerry avoided the question. "She's in Chicago," was all he said.

A strange answer, if you considered it. It was a second answer to tell her his parents were separated. That was more important to Jerry than defining his mother. First things first. A really smart boy, Jerry was.

"Toasted cheese sandwiches," Lorna announced. "My specialty. And a salad. And soup if you want it, Jerry, right out of a can. Mrs. Bailey does most of the cooking. Today she's getting Dad ready." She might as well tell Jerry ahead of time. "Dad is still wobbly on his legs," she added.

Jerry heard a funny kind of noise, like a wheelchair that needed oil. A door that he guessed led to the big room opened beyond the table, and Paul Bernard stood in the doorway. Mrs. Bailey stood behind him, her hands on his hips.

As Mr. Bernard took a step toward him, Jerry heard the sound again. He stood up and instinctively moved toward Mr. Bernard. He didn't look too steady on his aluminum crutches, thrusting out one squeaky foot, then the next.

Paul Bernard extended his hand. "Welcome to Oz, Jerry Huffaker. I am the Tin Man, as you are bound to have noticed at once. Dorothy is at the stove. Holding me steady as I go is the witch of—which witch are you anyway, Mrs. Bailey?"

"I don't know what you're saying, Mr. Bernard. I don't read your books," Mrs. Bailey snapped. "Let's take the chair there on your left."

"That's *The Wizard of Oz*," Jerry spoke up. He was surprised to hear his voice. "Where's Toto? He has to be with Dorothy."

The great man eased himself into the chair. He grimaced. "The witch of wherever has turned him into sea lions. You said you weren't much of a reader, Jerry. I said you were."

"I didn't read it," Jerry confessed. "I've seen the movie a couple of times on television. Mom and I liked to watch it."

Lorna laughed. "You're out of touch, Dad. Kids don't have to read these days, do they, Mrs. Bailey? They just have to look."

"Marsha was a reader. I made my boys read, too, I can tell

you, when they were growing up. Not that it ever did them any good," she sniffed. "As soon as they left school neither one of them picked up a book."

"Here comes lunch," Lorna said. She put plates in front of her father, Mrs. Bailey, and Jerry. "I gave you white bread, Jerry, and the rest of us brown bread. Do you want potato chips or corn chips?"

"Corn chips, thanks." Mr. Bernard was staring at him with a half smile on his face that made Jerry uneasy. He knew from last Saturday that the smile meant Mr. Bernard was going to ask him a strange question. But the smile disappeared, and it was a serious question this time.

"You live with your father, do you, Jerry?"

"Yes, sir." Jerry didn't feel like going on. He had already told Lorna where Mom was.

"I lived with my father, too, when I was in my teens and afterward for a while when I came home from college and started to write."

Mr. Bernard's expression changed again. He set his lips hard. He held his sandwich poised halfway between his mouth and the plate. He wasn't looking at Jerry anymore.

"My mother died when I was thirteen," he suddenly continued. "After that, it was only Dad and I. You know what's bothering me now, Jerry?"

"No, sir."

"I don't even have a picture of her. Not of Dad, either. We were too poor to own a camera. There's only one family picture, and that's of me. It's hard to remember what they looked like. It's easier to recall what they wore and what they said and what they did. What they looked like, that's the hard part now."

Maybe the interview had begun. Jerry wasn't sure. Mrs.

Bailey wasn't paying much attention. Lorna was poking at her salad, picking out the avocado slices and pushing them to one side of her plate. Mr. Bernard must have been talking only to him.

"I have a lot of pictures of Mom," he said. "She kept an album. Now Dad and I have begun a new one for her. I'll take it to Chicago after Christmas."

Lorna smiled secretly. Jerry's mother was a Mom. That was good, she figured. Boys who called their mothers Mom, according to her theory, generally loved their mothers a lot. And Dad, what did *he* call his mother? He had never said. She must have been more than "my mother." Lorna waited. She had a notion she was going to have the answer pretty soon.

"The strap on the left is pulled too tight," Paul Bernard complained. "It hurts when I sit down. Could you make it looser tomorrow?"

"It has to be tight, Paul," Mrs. Bailey replied, "or the whole thing might come off. You'll get used to it again. The strap will loosen up. I suppose we could send it back to the company or have one of their men come here to take a look at it."

"You see what a complicated mechanism I am wearing, Jerry. There are technicians to adjust them and repair them. You would think I'm a racing car. All we're talking about is a couple of fake legs."

Jerry didn't know what to say. What Mr. Bernard was saying sounded personal to him, very personal. It made him feel uncomfortable.

"Well," he said, "they must be better than the wheelchair sometimes. You must get bored with it."

"No, I never have. Once I made up my mind that's what it

had to be, it didn't bother me. You don't need legs to sit at a desk and write. But this week I had a crazy idea. I wanted to walk outside again. Walk, not be pushed. You were telling Lorna how fine it was out there on the cliff, and that reminded me of another place in another time and the idea came to me that I had to go out there myself, standing up, not sitting down, but standing up on my fake legs. It was time to walk out to the cliffs again, I told myself, and see what my two old friends down below were doing."

Mr. Bernard remembered he was still holding a cheese sandwich halfway up to his mouth. He took a bite and started in on his salad. He ate quickly, Jerry noticed, like the kids at school who had a short lunch break and didn't want to use it all up eating.

Again, Jerry wondered where the talk about legs was leading. It certainly wasn't anything he could put in the *Scripture*, although Jake would probably find it interesting. Was Mr. Bernard getting it out of the way before he settled down to talking about what he did and the story of his life and whatever it was that made an interview any good?

Dad said he thought that was what you were expected to find out, the inside stuff. If you were a really good interviewer, he said, you asked questions that made the person talk about what was in back of all the easy stuff. What was going on now seemed to him to be inside out. He wished Mr. Bernard would move on to the easy stuff. Maybe they could deal with his legs later.

The great man stuffed the last shreds of lettuce into his mouth. He emptied the little glass of wine. "That was good, Lorna," he said. "Thank you."

"You eat more here at the table than you do from your tray," Lorna observed.

"That's because I use up three or four thousand calories stumping out here. Okay, Mrs. Bailey, let's get me up."

Paul Bernard turned around in his chair and reached for his crutches. With Mrs. Bailey's help he lurched upward, tottering for a moment before he gained control. Looking down at Jerry, he said, "I'm ready. Let's walk out to the cliffs and see what's going on."

11

———— ◆ ————

ALONE, PAUL BERNARD MADE HIS WAY CLOSE TO THE EDGE of the cliff. Jerry stood beside him. Bernard put his hand on Jerry's shoulder for support. Together, they gazed down the slope of the cliff. Today the sea lions were turned around and looking out to sea.

"They don't like the sun all that much," Bernard told Jerry. "They get sunburned. They have to go into the water and cool off."

As he spoke, one of the sea lions crawled into the ocean. It disappeared under the water and surfaced beside a flat rock. The other sea lion watched, then put its head down and went back to sleep.

"Is that the male out in the water?" Jerry asked.

"Yes. He's getting along in years, like me. But he's still strong enough to chase the young bulls away. We call him Harpo. His wife is Mom."

Jerry thought he had better get started with the interview. "How long have you lived here?" he asked.

The great man wasn't listening. He was leaning forward on his crutches, looking out across the sluggish surf and the whitecaps beyond. He was breathing deeply. Jerry could see his heavy chest rise and fall beneath the windbreaker. A faint smile came slowly to his lips. He said a few silent words to himself.

Then he turned toward Jerry. "I heard you, Jerry. I was thinking of the place where I grew up. It wasn't much like this, I suppose, but sometimes when I stand here, with all the years between, I can't tell the difference.

"How long have I been here? Let me see. Just about thirty years. I went to San Francisco to get my tin legs and to learn how to use them. Some hospital people drove me down the coast to see the sights. We came up the county road. There was a dirt road up to the cliff here and I made them take me up. It was like another dirt road I once knew. They pushed my chair over to the cliff here. Right away, I knew this was where I had to be. I never went back east. Let's go sit on the deck, Jerry. I'm starting to wear out."

As they started the ascent, Lorna and Mrs. Bailey moved close in behind Paul Bernard. Slowly, throwing out one squeaky leg in front of the other, Bernard made his way back up the path. His face was flushed. Sweat rolled down his rugged cheeks. His teeth were fiercely set. On the deck he let himself fall into a sturdy tube-and-canvas chair.

"I made it, Lorna," he crowed. "You said I wouldn't make it the first week."

"I should have known you would, Dad," Lorna replied. "You pretty much always do what you say you're going to do." She looked at Jerry. "He was just showing off for you, Jerry."

"I know," Jerry said. "That makes me feel good. I'm glad Mr. Bernard did it."

What a strange boy, Lorna thought again. It was like Jerry was way ahead of them. She looked at her father to see if he had noticed. He had, of course. He was smiling that self-satisfied smile that told her he knew all the while what Jerry was thinking.

Mrs. Bailey pushed the wheelchair across the deck. "You had better have this, Paul," she told the great man. "It gives you more support. Do you want to keep those things on a while longer, or shall I take them off?"

"Oh, I'll stay hitched up a while longer. Thank you, Mrs. Bailey. Anyway, it's Saturday. What are you doing up here on the weekend?"

"I'm here most weekends, if you notice, Paul," Mrs. Bailey said. "I'm like you and Lorna. I don't have anywhere to go. I live in Smithville," she explained to Jerry. "I guess I don't really live there. I have a little house there. I used to think Paul here needed me all the time. Then I discovered he's one of those men who don't need anyone; but I stay around anyway. The truth is I like it better up here than down in town. I'm going inside. You give a holler when you want in, Paul."

We're all explaining ourselves to Jerry, it occurred to Lorna. Mrs. Bailey had never said that to her, even though Lorna knew it was so. Mrs. Bailey's daughter and her family now lived in the little house and Mrs. Bailey went to visit, but she lived here on the cliff with the other outcasts.

"Sit down, Jerry," Bernard commanded. "You can have my chair. It will help you understand what I have to put up with."

"Dad!" Lorna protested. "I'll go get Jerry a chair."

But Jerry Huffaker had already put himself down in the

steel chair. He moved his body around in it. He tested the wheel and the brake. "This is neat," he said. "I've always wanted to sit in one of these chairs at the airport. But Mom said I shouldn't—they were for the invalids and old people." He stopped and looked at the great man. "I'm sorry, Mr. Bernard. Well, you know what I mean."

"Indeed, I do," Bernard replied. "When my mother was in the hospital, I'd go to visit. If she was in bed, I'd sit in her wheelchair. It was an old wooden thing with a straw seat and a straw back, I recall, and you couldn't steer it. That was the nurse's job. For some reason, I wanted that chair for myself. Maybe it was because I didn't have a bike, I'm not sure. Maybe I even asked Dad for it when my mother died. Well, I got myself one soon enough, didn't I?"

Jerry didn't reply. Lorna held her hand to her eyes. "There's a tanker going down the coast," she announced, "a big one."

The great man was silent for a while. He rearranged his memories to tell Jerry Huffaker about the big white house and how he and it came to be there. It wasn't much to tell, but he could see that Jerry might be more interested in the house and the cliffs and the fat sea lions than he was in the world's greatest writer. The thought reassured Bernard.

"I was telling you about the house," he began. "Not the house at first, but the place. Property along the coast wasn't very expensive then. Anyway, I was rich, very rich. I used to write best sellers, Jerry. I didn't write them to be best sellers, you understand. I wrote them, and that's what they got to be. I can't tell you why, because I never understood it. I've always written only to please myself.

"Anyway, I got a lawyer, and he bought the property. I got an architect and told him what I wanted. Nothing fancy, just a big square house with an upstairs and a deck and a lot of glass. And I told him I wanted it in a hurry. I was stuck in this hotel in San Francisco where I couldn't write and couldn't move, with a gorilla of a nurse who was teaching me to walk again."

Jerry remembered his dad had said he thought the Bernard home had once won a prize and was a historic building. He asked Paul if this was so.

Bernard nodded. "You know what that crazy architect did before he started to work, Jerry? He read the books I had written. He told me that later. You know what else he did? He found out from Meredith—my ex-wife; you already know that, don't you?—where I grew up and he went to have a look at that. 'I had to know what you wanted before I started, Mr. Bernard,' he told me.

"I didn't know what I wanted myself, just a big square house where I could look out and see to the edge of nowhere. But this architect understood. It was his first big job, I guess. He lived in a tent up here and saw to it that it was done just the way he planned it."

Bernard looked at Lorna, who was listening intently. He realized he had never told Lorna the details of the big white house. Why hadn't he? he asked himself. It wasn't part of the forbidden land. But it was, it certainly was. It was on the road past the NO TRESPASSING sign. Once started down that road, he understood, there was no turning back. And he was started down it. Wheelchair or tin legs, he was headed back. Well, there was no help for it now. They had let this kid into his life, and one way or another, they all belonged to him, even Mrs. Bailey.

"When it was done, Jerry, you know what that crazy architect did? He had an ambulance bring me down. They parked at the county road. He made the gorilla push me up the road to the house, that whole crooked mile of road. He helped the gorilla push. What did *you* think when you saw this place last Saturday, Jerry?"

"I had to think about it, sir," Jerry replied. "I went home and tried to explain to Dad, but I couldn't. I decided it was the greatest house I'd ever seen."

"That's what I thought, too. The architect said he was pretty sure it was what I wanted. He folded his tent and went away. He came back a year later with some other architects. They spent the day looking around and gave him a prize. Lorna told me that it is a landmark now. Your dad was right."

"Is it like where you grew up?" Jerry asked.

"That's another question, isn't it, Jerry? You'll need another answer for that one."

12

IT WASN'T EXACTLY AN ANSWER THAT PAUL BERNARD GAVE Jerry; it was more of a remembering. Later, sitting in the living room, where he and Dad seldom went after his mother left, Jerry tried to tell his father about what Mr. Bernard had said. "It's confusing, Dad. I mean, I understood what he was saying all right, but I couldn't keep track of where he was and when and, you know, stuff I can't explain."

"I think I understand, Jerry," his father said. "That is apparently how he writes these days. It's what makes him so difficult for some people, including me, to read. I suppose it's also what makes him the great man folks say he is. They call it 'Bernard's style.' You just have to be patient with him."

What a heavy load to lay on a young teenager, Ted Huffaker thought. Should he suggest to Jerry that he suspend his visits for a while? It was clear that Bernard was using Jerry for some purpose of his own. He decided he'd wait and see. Jerry was mature in many ways. If Amy were here, she'd tell him kids were a lot tougher emotionally than they used to be. Perhaps he should call her. He hadn't dared since the day she stormed out of the house to the taxi. She called and talked to Jerry on Sunday afternoons, and Jerry told him what she had said. He was pretty sure Jerry told Amy how his father was getting along. The first month she wrote a couple of times, fat envelopes probably full of explanations, but he didn't open them. He hurt too much.

After the turmoil of the last year, he knew his son could look after himself, but these Saturday visits were something different. Bernard was obviously a strange and powerful man. Jerry would need to tell what went on in the big white house with the man who talked literature. "You were out on the deck all afternoon, Jerry? And Lorna was there, too?" he asked.

"Yes, we were on the deck, the three of us," Jerry told him.

When the sun was about an hour from going down, Mrs. Bailey had come out with two glasses of wine and a root beer and a plate of cheese and crackers. "Your supper is on the stove," she told them. "It's nothing but chili. Lorna can warm up the tortillas. I ought to go to town and see how Marsha is getting along. Maybe I'll spend the night there. You make Lorna take you home, Jerry. The maniacs take their cars out Saturday nights. The roads aren't safe for anybody."

Lorna had drunk her wine and stood up. "Shall we say good-night to Harpo and Mom, Jerry? How about you, Dad? Stretch your legs again?"

Paul Bernard laughed. "You have your mother's nasty tongue, Lorna." Suddenly, he felt tired. Too much sun and fresh air and far too much talk. He wasn't used to that. "We'll go in when the sun sets, Jerry."

The sea lions were gone. The tide was pushing in over the rocks toward the cliff. The surface of the ocean shimmered in the late afternoon sun. Fifty feet from the shore, Lorna saw a head pop up. "Look out there, Jerry," she said. "It's Harpo. He wants to say good-night." She waved and shouted. "Good-night, you lazy Harpo." The head disappeared.

"Some days," she told Jerry, "those guys are the only ones I have to talk to. Dad is writing and Mrs. Bailey is in one of her moods. I come out here to sit down and shout at the sea lions. I swear they know what I am saying. Every once in a while they bark at me. What do you think, Jerry? Do they understand or do they think I'm going to throw them a fish?"

"They don't have anyone else to talk to, either," Jerry observed.

"They have each other," Lorna pointed out.

"Maybe," Jerry answered. "It's hard to tell what's going on sometimes. Mom and Dad had each other, but it didn't do them much good. The last couple of years they didn't talk unless they were quarreling."

"Was it awful for you?" Lorna asked.

Jerry shrugged. "Not really, I guess. You crawl down inside yourself and hope things will get better, but you know they won't. You get used to the idea that sooner or later something has to happen and you wait for that, and then you sort of hope it will happen soon so you can crawl back out."

"Are you out now?"

"Probably. It's hard for me to know what it was like before. But Dad is all right, and that's good. He's the one who really got hurt. He lost my mother. I didn't."

Jerry omitted that part of the afternoon talk as he spoke to his father. "We went back to the deck and watched the sun go down. It's a special time for Mr. Bernard and Lorna. You're not supposed to say anything. Then we went inside and ate our chili. Lorna put my bike in the trunk and brought me home."

Lorna had also called. She apologized, Ted remembered. She said they had talked the afternoon away, forgetting about the time; Jerry had eaten a bowl of chili with them. A cultured Eastern voice, he supposed, but not patronizing. It was an accent, nothing more. In fact, it sounded friendly enough. Half an hour later, car lights outside and then scraping of a bike lifted from a trunk. He went to the door and a happy voice came from the car. "Here he is, Mr. Huffaker, safe and sound. Thank you for the loan of him."

They had gone to the Dairy Queen again. Now they sat in the unused living room. Ted fumbled with his thoughts. Amy would have known what to say. "What do you mean, there wasn't any where or when?" he finally asked, trying to draw Jerry back into the afternoon's experience.

"You know, Dad, how in a dream there isn't any beginning, it's just there, and maybe you're part of it and maybe you're just watching. And there isn't much of an end, you just wake up. Well, that's how Mr. Bernard was talking. It wasn't like a nightmare or anything, and it wasn't always that interesting, except to Lorna. But you see, Dad, Jake Wilson sent me up there as a reporter, and when I tried to get ahold of what I had to write about, I couldn't. Do you understand, Dad?"

His father nodded. "You couldn't call it an interview, could you? Did you ask questions?"

"Oh, yes, I did. Mr. Bernard is easy to talk to. He's very polite. He would shut up and look at me to see if I had anything to say. Lorna would interrupt to ask him something or tease him, and we would all stop and talk together, the three of us, and then Mr. Bernard would talk again."

"But some of it wasn't interesting to you? Was it hard for you to understand?"

"No, not really. It was that I got left behind in what he said, left out, sort of, and I wasn't sure sometimes I should be listening. Sometimes Mr. Bernard seemed to be talking to himself, or maybe to Lorna."

"Was it embarrassing to you? Was it too personal, something you felt was none of your business?"

"No, no, nothing like that. It was like sections of a dream. You wake up and all you can remember is part of what you dreamed. There was a lot more that you want to remember, but you can't. You're stuck with only one part, and it may not even be the best part."

"And when you asked Mr. Bernard a question?"

"I got an answer. I asked him where he grew up. He wanted to know if I had ever heard of some place called the Eastern Shore. I said no. Mr. Bernard said he didn't have a map around, and it didn't matter, that the important thing was that the Eastern Shore was very special to people who lived there. Do you know where it is, Dad?"

"More or less. It's half the state of Maryland. It's a long peninsula between the Chesapeake Bay and the Atlantic Ocean. It's like Baja California."

"That's what Paul, I mean Mr. Bernard, said. He asked me if I knew where New York and Washington were, and he said it was between them on the map. He said that when he was growing up it was a very poor and very beautiful place."

"Most of what he told you was about growing up there? Are you going back next Saturday? If you are, you could talk to Jake before then. Ask him if Mr. Bernard ever wrote about the Eastern Shore. Then you could read and ask him questions for the interview."

There were a lot of problems with what Dad had just said. Jerry thought he'd better deal with them one by one.

"Mr. Bernard expects me back. He didn't exactly say so, but he does. But I don't feel right about it, Dad. Saturdays and Sundays are our days together. What do you think?"

"I think I'm proud, Jerry, prouder than I can say, and your mother will be proud, too, that Paul Bernard wants to talk to our son when he refuses to give anyone else the time of day. We'll have lots of Saturdays later, Jerry. If the ride is too much, I'll take you up in the Toyota."

"No. The ride is fine. Lorna said she'd come pick me up when it was rainy. You see, Dad, I don't know when he's ever going to finish. Lorna told me what he wants to write about is his growing up. He never has. She says it's very important for him now to be able to do it. Now he has something she calls writer's block. He's never had it before."

"Well, Jerry, I'd like it if we could set aside Saturday nights to talk about Mr. Bernard and his writer's block. It will help me with my teaching. I only know about writers through what they write. Will you do that?"

"That's fine, Dad. What about Mr. Wilson?"

"Why don't you tell him you're still getting acquainted and you haven't done a real interview? You can tell him you forgot to take a notebook with you. That's true, isn't it?"

"It's true, all right, but there's a problem with that."

"What's the problem?"

"This afternoon Mr. Bernard said a couple of things I wanted to write down so I wouldn't forget them—nothing very personal—and I said I hadn't brought my notebook with me. I asked Lorna for a pad and pencil. 'Don't bother about that,' Mr. Bernard said. 'I'll write the interview for you as we go along. How about that, Jerry?'"

13

JAKE WILSON DIDN'T WAIT UNTIL WEDNESDAY TO CORNER
Jerry. Bright and early Monday morning, Jake was waiting
for him when history class got out. Jerry didn't have his excuses ready.

"How did it go, Jerry? Do you have a big story for us?"

Jerry looked at his watch. "Gee, I'm not sure I have time
to talk to you now, Jake."

"You have a free period, Jerry. I looked at your schedule.
So do I. Let's go to the lunchroom. I'll buy you a Coke."

"I'd like to, Jake, but I have to get ready for math. I didn't
finish the assignment."

"I'm not going to take all hour, Jerry. I'm beginning to
think you're avoiding me for some reason." He put his arm
around Jerry's shoulder and marched him to the lunchroom.

"Now, what's going on?" he asked, pushing a can of Coke
toward Jerry. "Do you understand that you may be working

on the hottest literary story in the whole country, maybe the whole world? I'm not kidding. Nobody, but nobody, has gotten close to Bernard for years, since he moved into his castle down the coast. Maybe no one got close to him even before that, for all I know. So, Jerry boy, spill the beans."

"Well," Jerry began, trying to sort out what was true and what would protect him from Mr. Wilson, who wasn't going to leave him alone—he could see that. "Well, it wasn't really an interview, we just talked."

"Oh, you just talked. That may be better than an interview. What did you talk about? Did he let his hair down, Jerry? Whatever he said, it's bound to be news, because no one else has ever heard it."

"We talked about the sea lions who live at the bottom of the cliff and about the big house." Jerry told himself to stay away from the topic of Paul's legs. "And we talked a little about where he grew up."

Jake wasn't too interested in that. "It's back east, in Maryland. We know that. He was a farm boy, wasn't he?"

"Yes," Jerry answered.

"And he was a foot soldier in the Second World War, in Germany and Japan, is that right?"

"I don't know. He didn't say anything about that."

"Well, he was. That's public record. We know that much about his life. It's the rest of it that's closed. We have only the outline."

"Mr. Bernard said he was poor, the family, I mean. His mother died when he was thirteen. His father brought him up the rest of the way, he said."

"Yes, yes," Jake said impatiently. "He came back home from the war and finished school at some hick college on the Eastern Shore. He lived with his father on the farm and wrote his first book. It was a big, tough book about the war with a crazy title, *Journey to the Bitter End*. It was the best war book ever written in this country. It was made into a movie and translated into fifty-seven different languages or something. Overnight, he was rich and famous."

"Yes," Jerry said. Keep on talking, Mr. Wilson, he said to himself, keep on talking.

"Old Bernard told you that? Good, Jerry. You were being a reporter. Now we're moving ahead."

"He said he wrote a book which was a best seller and it made a lot of money." It was all right to tell Mr. Wilson that, since he already knew it. Jake already knew a lot of things Mr. Bernard hadn't told Jerry. He wouldn't have to be so careful if Jake did most of the talking. Jerry sipped his Coke and looked down at his watch. Only half an hour to go. It was a good thing he had almost finished his math home-work—all but the last problem, which he didn't understand.

Mr. Wilson was talking again. "He wrote two or three books right after that: a book about some biblical figures and a strange book, *The Land Beyond*, about somewhere no one could figure out. They were different, but they sold. Did he tell you that?"

"Sort of. Mr. Bernard said he didn't set out to write best sellers, but they ended up being best sellers. He said he only wrote to please himself." Was it all right to tell Jake that, too?

"There you go, Jerry, you really did your job. That's good stuff for your interview. Wonderful!"

"Dad said *The Land Beyond* was hard to read. We have a copy."

"All Bernard's books are hard to read. That's the remark-able thing about him, as far as I can see. After you told me you were going back, I started reading some of his stuff I hadn't read. Each one is more difficult than the one before. Not hard to follow—Bernard isn't a surrealist—just difficult, mind you. He makes the reader think about himself in ways that are uncomfortable and even unacceptable. And, of course, he writes like an angel. No one in this country has ever written English the way Paul Bernard writes it. That's why they gave him the Nobel. They should have done that years ago. It's a disgrace. What did he say about the Nobel Prize?"

"Nothing much. He didn't mention it. I did, but he just laughed and said he got it because he managed to stay alive in a wicked world for sixty-five years."

"He said that? Jerry, you're the greatest. This is going to make the *Scripture* a best seller, too. When can we have the interview?"

It was going to be difficult, after all. Jerry sneaked another look at his watch. Fifteen minutes to go. He would try to stall. "What I don't understand, Jake, is how his books are best sellers if they're so difficult. I don't like to read hard stuff in English class. Dad said he had trouble reading what Bernard wrote and gave up after one book. He didn't actually say that, but it's what he meant."

"Me, too, Jerry, just like your dad. I read a couple, the big war book and another one whose title I can't remember, something about Indians. The fact is, your dad and I don't have time to go slow. We have classes and homework and meetings and school newspapers and tennis coaching and soccer and all that. We don't have time to read slow. It's a shame, because we ought to."

"But—" Jerry began to ask his question again.

"I know what you're going to say. Some people, I'm sure,

buy his books to be fashionable. They are literary snobs. Whether they read them is something else. All the libraries buy his books because he is an American classic and they have to. And, finally, I understand to my surprise, there are still a whole lot of people around the world who want to read slow, who want to admire how he writes, who want to be troubled by what he writes. Some people would rather read a book by Paul Bernard than watch television. You've interviewed a real genius, Jerry. You ought to be proud of yourself. Now, when can we have your story?"

Mr. Wilson looked at his watch. "I have to go to class in five minutes. By the end of the week? We're setting up the October edition. We'll give you the whole front page."

It had come down to what Jerry had feared it would come down to. "Gee, I don't know, Jake. I don't think I can. I haven't finished."

"What do you mean, you haven't finished? Didn't you talk to old Bernard on Saturday?"

"Yes, I did, but I have to go back next Saturday. Maybe some other Saturdays. I guess I haven't finished. Mr. Bernard asked me to come back."

Disbelief passed over Jake Wilson's face. In a slow, subdued voice, he said, "Let me get this straight, Jerry. You're going back on Saturday and perhaps the Saturday after that. Is that what you said?"

"I think so, Mr. Wilson. I guess that's what Mr. Bernard wants me to do."

Mr. Wilson didn't notice he wasn't a Jake anymore. "How long were you there Saturday?"

Jerry made a pretense of counting on his fingers, anything to stall until the bell for the next hour's classes. "Let's see. I got there just before lunch, say twelve o'clock, and Lorna must have brought me home about seven, right after supper. Six or seven hours, I'd say." Jerry pushed his chair back to stand up. "I have my math class. Miss Reynolds said something about a quiz."

"Sit back down, Jerry." Jake Wilson's voice was tight and hard. "This is more important than your math class and my English class. Let's get it straight. You talked to Paul Bernard for seven hours. Did I hear you correctly?"

"Six, maybe," Jerry agreed. "And Lorna. She was there, too. She talked a lot. Maybe not so much, but a good deal."

"Yes, Lorna, old Bernard's daughter. And the Saturday before," Mr. Wilson asked suspiciously. "What about then? Did you see him?"

Jerry's heart began to hammer. He was in for it. Dad wouldn't want him to lie outright. Avoid a question maybe, the way Dad used to do when Mom was pressing him about something, but stick as close to the truth as you can. Jerry took the last swallow from the can.

"Actually, I did, but I'm not too clear about what went on."

"But you did get an interview last week and you didn't tell me about it. Why not? Is there something going on that I should know about?" Jake squinted at Jerry. "Did your dad say you should save it for a big paper in San Francisco?"

"Of course not. Dad would never do that. Look, Mr. Wilson, I have to go. Miss Reynolds gets mad when we don't show up for a quiz. The first day Mr. Bernard and Lorna just asked me in for some hot cocoa because I had come a long way and it was chilly outside. I had to push my bike a mile up the road. We only talked about the two sea lions. Afterward I guess he felt bad about the interview, and he asked me back. That's about it, Mr. Wilson. I have to go. I really do."

"And why does he want you back?" Jake insisted.

"I don't know. Honestly, I don't know."

"Neither do I, Jerry." Mr. Wilson laughed, except it didn't sound much like a laugh. "Go on to your quiz. Tell Miss Reynolds I kept you overtime. Friday, Jerry, this coming Friday, right here at this time, we'll have another talk. Don't forget, Jerry. I'll be waiting for you, same time, same station. Don't forget, understand?"

14

PAUL BERNARD WAS BACK AT HIS DESK. AS LORNA DRANK
her morning coffee and watched him from across the room,
he wrote briefly, stopped, pushed his chair away from the
desk, turned toward the ocean, and read what he had written. He smiled to himself and turned back to the desk.

He sensed that Lorna was watching. He wheeled himself
over to the sofa. "Were you spying on me, Lorna?"

"Not spying exactly, Dad, just keeping track of what
you're up to. You don't seem to be your old, grumpy self
these days. I actually heard you humming yesterday afternoon. I'm curious. You're writing again, aren't you?"

"I wouldn't call it writing. I'm putting down things I might
be able to use later." Bernard moved closer to the sofa. He
nodded at the sketches Lorna had made yesterday on the
cliff. "And you, Lorna, what are *you* up to? I noticed you
had your camera out, too. Getting ready to go back to work,
are you?"

"I thought I might free-lance. I haven't done anything for a long time except fuss at you and help Mrs. Bailey."

"You'll be leaving?" There was concern in Bernard's voice.

"Of course not, Dad. I just got here," she teased. "Go back to your desk. I like to see you write when you enjoy it. When you're having trouble, I can feel the tension all the way over here in my cave."

Bernard reached out to Lorna's hand. He squeezed it hard and rolled to his desk. Lorna wondered whether she should have asked him what he was writing. She never had. Eventually he would tell her; well, not tell her, but read a page or two he was particularly pleased with. And when he didn't, she'd sneak a couple of yellow sheets out of the basket before Mrs. Bailey emptied it. These pages were all she knew about Dad's work until the author's copies of a finished book arrived and sat unopened on the corner of his desk until Mrs. Bailey or she, scissors in hand, asked, "Do you want me to open these?"

Her father would nod without lifting his eyes from the yellow pad, and Lorna or Mrs. Bailey would cut the tape, unwrap the books, and make two stacks on the same corner of his desk. A few days later, Lorna, never Mrs. Bailey, would complete the ritual. She would carry them upstairs to Dad's study and put them on the bookshelf, next to the other piles.

Then and only then, Lorna would take a copy to her room. There she read it slowly, word by word, sentence by sentence, searching, hoping, for a mention of her existence. No matter how disguised it was, she was confident she would recognize herself. When she had finished, disappointed and hurt, she returned the book to the top of the pile.

Lorna had pored over more than thirty years' worth of

books, fourteen by actual count, looking for an acknowledgement of her existence. Not a trace of Wife Meredith or Daughter Lorna did she find. At first, she told herself she couldn't blame him. Wife and child had disappeared from his life. Legless and angry, he must have cut them both from memory.

Lorna could understand that, but you would think that when she started to visit him—at her insistence, never his invitation—he would accept her in his writing as well as in his castle. And when she finally fled a pointless life back East to join Dad in his splendid isolation, she had a right to expect a welcoming sentence or two in one of those manuscripts he sent off to his publishers.

Lorna took her pad and drew a dark, whiskered, popeyed face. Dad knew as much about Harpo as he did about her. He had even put the two stupid sea lions in one of his novels, not only put them in but built a couple of chapters around them. That thought always made her angry. I gave up my mother and my career and Tony to retire in this forsaken corner of the California coast to look after you, she thought, and I'm not as important to you as a couple of sea lions named Harpo and Mom. Sternly, she looked across to the desk. Dad was smiling again. It was good to see him happy. Against her will, she smiled to herself and admitted, as she always did when she arrived at this point, that what she told herself was not so.

She hadn't left her mother, not ever. She never had the chance. Meredith had left her daughter, left her with nannies and her grandparents and Meredith's sister and at boarding schools and at college. Lorna understood even then that, by default, she was bound to be her father's child, and that was long before she got up the courage to visit him.

And she didn't give up much of a career, if you could call sketching and photographing skinny fashion models a career. And she didn't give up Tony; she'd never had him. He was only the last in a series of men she had met and turned away from.

What is wrong? Lorna asked herself. Why am I going back to things that really don't matter? Am I working myself into a state so I'll have a reason to walk out on Dad? To go back to something familiar or move on to try something different? And why now, when Dad and I are closer than we've ever been?

Lorna didn't have to answer herself. She already knew. She was jealous. Not hurt, the way she was each time she finished one of her father's novels. She was just plain jealous of a fourteen-year-old kid whom *she*, not Dad, had brought into the house. Anger flared up as she remembered that Dad had told Jerry Huffaker more about himself on two Saturday afternoons than he had confided to her in seven years of living in the same house. What was he doing over there at his desk now, smiling to himself like a satisfied cat as he wrote down his conversations with a stranger who had no claim at all to Paul Bernard's attentions? What was going on?

She knew the answer to that, too. Her father had to deal with himself before he could write again. As he had sent off his most recent manuscript to the publisher, he complained briefly to Lorna, "I'm drying up. I can't squeeze out another one."

Later, during the week of the Nobel crisis, as she called it, her father, in another uncharacteristic confession, had argued that it would not be honest to accept such a prize until he was confident that what he intended to do would have the value of what he had already done. And it was only yesterday, the two of them standing side by side above the sea lions' beach watching Harpo and Mom sleep, that Dad declared that the signs were coming down.

"What signs?" Lorna had asked.

"The signs in my head that have kept me from writing about what sooner or later I would have to write about."

"Which is?"

"These!" he shouted, banging his left tin leg with a crutch.

"It won't do you any good to keep after him about the accident, as he calls it," Meredith had said to Lorna when she told her mother she was moving out to Dad's big white house. "It's what drove me away, and if you persist in knowing, it will drive you away, too."

Meredith then reviewed for the last time the history of her marriage with Paul Bernard. Lorna knew it by heart. It never changed from one telling to the next. Nor was her mother's despair less genuine now than it must have been thirty years ago as she described how she was forced, "actually forced," to take her daughter and walk out on the crippled novelist. "It wasn't really that I had to know," Meredith explained. "It was that he refused to tell me."

Meredith had met Paul Bernard at a splashy publication party for Bernard's second book, the one about the prophet Jeremiah, of all things. She had brought a boyfriend. Drinking champagne, they laughed at the burly hick in his baggy suit and dimestore necktie. She had laughed, yes, but she left the party with the hick, not her fashionable boyfriend, and a month later she actually married him and went down to the Eastern Shore to live in a ramshackle old farmhouse not far from a wretched river she never did know the name of. "I stuck it out," she told Lorna. "I loved him so much I would have stayed with him anywhere.

"Your father wanted to move," she continued. "I didn't steal him away from the farm. I was pregnant and that farm was obviously no place to bring up a child. Your grandfather took it into his head that Paul and I were outcasts or something. He ignored us completely. We found a place in the city and Paul kept right on writing. He probably didn't even know we had moved."

"And me?" Lorna would always ask. "What did he do when I came along?"

"Oh, every once in a while he'd come up for air and hold you in his lap and tell me how much he loved us and apologize for neglecting us and go back to what he was doing. That wasn't much of a problem for me. I had looked after myself before Paul Bernard, and I looked after myself during Paul Bernard, and I have looked after myself after Paul Bernard. I am not hard to please. I had my own life, as I called it. But I think Paul and I would have made it if : . ."

Always the "if." A couple of times a year, Paul would head back home to be with his father, Lorna's grandfather, "a sad failure of a farmer who drank more than was good for him and never talked," in Meredith's words. He tended his fields with the help of an idiot farmboy and hunted and fished at the river.

Paul went home alone. "He understood I didn't think much of his dad." He went and came back. He didn't talk about the visits. "He never seemed to talk much about his father, but even I could see that they were attached to each other," Meredith confessed, "in ways that were deeper than his attachment to me."

Meredith came to the "if," also called "the accident." Paul had gone to the farm in September. One evening his father called Meredith. In a choking voice he told her that Paul had

had an accident and she had better come. He told her where the hospital was. She found Paul there, his legs gone. He had already been there a week.

The family doctor explained that Paul had lost both legs in an accident. He was reluctant to say what kind of an accident. In fact, he thereafter refused to discuss it. That was for Paul to explain. "Please don't ask me now," Paul beseeched her. "We'll talk about it later."

"He came home and, like always, he picked up right where he left off," Meredith said. "But with a difference. He wouldn't talk. He wouldn't talk about anything. He simply paid no attention to us." Not long after, his father died. Paul hired an ambulance for himself and went down to the farm alone. He came back as silent as ever; even more silent, if it was possible.

"I won't go into the rest of it, Lorna. You've heard it before. I am morally certain I did everything I could until it came to me that he was driving us away. There was nothing I could do. My love wasn't enough for him. We packed up and went. The last thing I said was, 'This is what you want, Paul. We're leaving. We can't take it anymore. Let me know if you need us.'

"All he said was, 'I'm sorry.' We never spoke again. He went off to California, and that was the end of it."

15

WHEN JERRY TOLD HIS FATHER ABOUT BEING CORNERED BY Jake, Ted was upset. "You're going to need some coaching before Friday. When Jake sinks his teeth into something . . . well . . . we'll talk about it Thursday night."

Ted did not go on to say, tempted though he was, that Jake Wilson was a selfish and frustrated teacher. He was beginning to see now that Wilson might very well pressure Jerry into giving him—not the *Scripture*, but *him*, Jake Wilson—the stories about Paul Bernard, which Wilson would use for his own advantage. Ted sensed from all his son had told him that Bernard and Jerry shared a confidence that Jerry wanted to honor. Bernard and Lorna seemed to be kind and decent people who had responded to Jerry the way Ted had seen other people respond to him. There was an almost instant feeling of affection for the quiet, almost shy boy who astonished people with his perceptive, off-beat observations. Ted often puzzled over how Jerry came to be the way he was. He did not recognize in Amy or himself the qualities that distinguished his son.

He was not the person to reveal the details of Jake Wilson's nasty side. Jerry might see it—rightly, Ted supposed—as a betrayal of his father's colleague. For better or worse, Wilson was a friend. Ted also knew it would be very much out of character for him to speak against Jake.

His ways weren't Amy's, however. She was more direct in personal matters, sometimes blunt, and, on occasion, profane. She could talk to Jerry with the objectivity that distance from the problem gave her. Also, she had a low opinion of Jake Wilson.

Should he call Amy? Was he brave enough yet to hear her voice and talk sensibly? It wasn't Amy he was afraid of, it was himself. At the thought of picking up the phone and dialing the number in Chicago, his chest began to hurt and his stomach to tighten.

But call Amy he did, late in the evening when he was certain Jerry was asleep.

"Hello, Ted," Amy said. "I was finishing up in the kitchen. My hands are still wet." A nervous little laugh, then, "How have you been?"

Ted was distracted by her greeting, and his fear turned to confusion. Was she, like him, covering up embarrassment?

"How have you been, Amy? It's good to hear your voice again." No need to be fearful any longer; he had begun. It was going to be all right. He felt strong enough now to explain. "I've been meaning to call and talk, but you know how it is with me. I had to straighten out some things in my head first. For a while when I heard you talking to Jerry Sunday afternoons, I had to go outside."

"It will be easy now, Ted. You've done it. I hope you'll call again. After all, we are still married." Another nervous little laugh. "Is something wrong with Jerry? He sounded all right on Sunday."

"Did he tell you what he's doing, Amy?" Ted asked. "He's actually interviewing Paul Bernard. Can you imagine? Bernard hasn't given an interview to anyone since the beginning of time, and our boy Jerry went right up to Bernard's door and knocked and they said come on in and take a seat. That's not quite how it happened, but no matter."

"He mentioned it. I felt it was still a private thing with him, and I didn't ask any questions. You know Jerry. He'll tell you when he has it all straight. He'll be a good journalist. I did tell him I would look forward to reading the interview in the *Scripture*. I read in the paper a while back that Bernard turned down the Nobel Prize."

"Jerry spent all Saturday at Bernard's house. They gave him lunch and supper and the daughter—that's Lorna— brought him home. He's made friends with a couple of sea lions down there. I wish you were here to listen to him when he comes home Saturday nights." Ted stopped. What have I said? he asked himself. "I mean, you ought to get Jerry to talk about it."

"Don't cover up, Ted. You can't cut our years together out of your life all at once. I'd be less than honest if I didn't say I wish I were there to share this with him, too. It will have to wait until Christmas."

"It can't, Amy," Ted blurted. "That's why I'm calling. At least, that's the first reason I'm calling you." He'd done it again. No more confessing. He gathered his thoughts into order and explained the problem—the potential problem, really—to Amy.

She listened. Once she broke in with a profanity Ted had

never approved of. Now it seemed appropriate. Amy didn't like Jake Wilson at all. Perhaps that's why I worked up the courage to call her, Ted thought. I wouldn't have to explain about Jake Wilson to Amy.

"You and Jerry do have a problem, Ted. I assume that what you want is what you haven't asked me yet to do, that is, let Jerry know about Jake's shortcomings and advise him on how to deal with the matter."

"Yes, if you would. Jerry and I are getting along fine and I, well, you know, this is your kind of business."

"Mother business or professional business, Ted?"

"Both, Amy. You have a better degree than I have for this."

"I'll think over what to say and call tomorrow night, Ted. You two guys can work out the strategy for dealing with Jake. Okay?"

"Okay, Amy, and thank you. Maybe I'll call to tell you how it went."

"I'd like to know. Take care, Ted."

"You, too, Amy."

Jerry was surprised to hear his mother's voice. His first thought was that something had happened. No, Mom just wanted to hear more about his interview with Paul Bernard. Her friend Stu had been telling her how eccentric the great man was.

Jerry assured her Mr. Bernard wasn't even a little bit strange except for his legs. The writer liked to tease Lorna and Jerry. He wasn't always certain what Mr. Bernard meant, but he was very nice about explaining himself. "I can see that people would bother him a lot if he would let them. If he did that, he wouldn't ever get his writing done."

That makes sense, Mom agreed. She asked him how the

writing was going. Jerry was slow to answer, then he said, "Mr. Bernard says he's going to write the interview."

"That does sound odd," his mother observed. "What does Jake think of that?"

"Well, I haven't told him. Dad said it might be a problem. He's going to coach me tomorrow night before I see Mr. Wilson on Friday. I guess Mr. Wilson can be difficult when he wants to be."

He can indeed, Mom told him. She went on to tell him a lot of other things about Mr. Wilson. Jerry wasn't altogether surprised. Kids in high school had told him that Mr. Wilson was moody and it paid to stay on his good side. If he had it in for you, he'd make your life miserable. He remembered Mr. Wilson's sudden anger Monday morning in the lunchroom.

"Your father will know what to do, Jerry. He probably wouldn't tell you everything I've told you, because he's not that sort of a person. He doesn't like to say bad things about people. You know me, Jerry; I don't mind at all, especially if what I say will help you stay out of trouble with Jake. Just be careful with him, Jerry. I love you. I'm counting the days until Christmas."

Thursday night Dad talked to him in a way he never had before. It was really grown-up talk, he decided, like the way Mr. Bernard and Lorna talked to him. It made Jerry feel important in a funny sort of way. It was a different father who was asking him questions and then more questions about the answers Jerry gave him. Dad was like Perry Mason in the big courtroom scenes.

"You have the feeling that what Mr. Bernard says is private, is that it, Jerry?"

"I think so, but he didn't say so."

"But he didn't say he was giving you material for the *Scripture*?"

"No."

"What did Lorna say when he told you he would write the interview?"

"Nothing right then. But on the way home she told me Mr. Bernard was slow getting started on his next book. I figured that maybe if he did something different, like writing about what he told me, he'd get started again."

"That was pretty shrewd, Jerry. What else did you figure out?"

"He wants to talk about when he was a kid like me, but he can't do it straight out. He's having a hard time. He starts telling me about the farm and the river and his dad, then he branches off into something else that's not part of that."

"What about his legs?"

"He laughs about them. Being a cripple doesn't bother him. He says he's used to it by now. He made a joke. He said he wouldn't be where he is if he had legs."

"What about Jake? What should we tell him? What did your mother say?"

"She told me to be careful, that Mr. Wilson could be mean if he wanted to. I already know that," Jerry answered. "The kids at school warned me."

"What should we do if he comes down hard on you to tell him everything about Mr. Bernard? That's the real problem, isn't it?"

"I can't run, that's for sure. It was Mr. Wilson's idea that I go up there in the first place. I can tell him Mr. Bernard is writing the interview, not me, and we'll have to wait."

"He won't wait, Jerry. He'll want it now. He's thinking that if he has some of the Bernard material he can escape from Santa Juana. He doesn't want to be here; he never has. He wants to be in San Francisco. He doesn't know when Mr. Bernard will finish or whether he will actually do it. Jake has come across a fantastic opportunity. It's what Mr. Bernard is telling you that's important now to him. I'm sure he's figuring *he* can write it up and *he* will be famous. It will be the story of his student, yes, who got in to see the great man, but it will be Jake Wilson's story. He sees a touch of fame for himself. Did your mother tell you that?"

"Yes. She said you'd know what to do."

"If it gets rough, Jerry, tell him to come and see me. If he gets ugly, walk out. Okay, Jerry?"

"Okay, Dad. We'll see how it goes."

16

IT DIDN'T GO WELL FROM THE START. MR. WILSON WAS waiting for Jerry at a table in the far corner of the lunchroom. He was scowling at a cup of coffee. He made a big show of looking at his watch. "Where have you been, Jerry boy? I can't spend my life waiting for cub reporters to check in."

Jerry had told himself to keep cool, no matter what. And don't speak out of turn, Dad had said. "Let Jake do the talking. Answer him honestly, but if it's something that Mr. Bernard wouldn't want you to talk about, don't. Use your own good sense, son. That's all I can tell you."

"Mrs. Aragon was giving out assignments for our papers. She hadn't finished by the bell. I came straight down here afterward."

"Did you tell her you had an important appointment with me?"

"No, sir. It's only a few minutes after ten now."

"Don't tell me what time it is. I have a watch. My watch tells me you're late. I said ten o'clock sharp."

Jerry didn't respond. Mr. Wilson was putting him in his place before he began to discuss the interview. He waited.

"Now that you're finally here, Jerry, I want you to know I've been thinking a lot about your interview with old Bernard."

Jerry decided that, no matter what, he wasn't going to listen to Jake Wilson call Mr. Bernard "old Bernard."

"Please, Mr. Wilson, could you call him 'Mr. Bernard' or 'Paul Bernard,' not 'old Bernard.' He's not so old."

"He's sixty-five years old, Jerry boy. That's old. If you don't mind, I'll call him what I please. I'm talking to you, not to him."

"Yes, but if you keep calling him that," Jerry protested, "I'm going to start seeing him that way, don't you understand, and then he'll be different when I talk to him. He'll be a different person, a kind of grandfather and not my friend. Names have a lot to do with how you feel about people."

"What do you call him when you're with him?" Mr. Wilson asked suspiciously.

"Mostly 'Mr. Bernard.' He said for me to call him 'Paul,' but it's hard for me to do that."

"Okay, Jerry, 'Mr. Bernard' it is. What I want to know now is, have you started keeping notes in a journal or something like that so when you start to write your story for the *Scripture* you'll have your material?"

Jerry shook his head. "The first day up there, I didn't expect him to see me. Last Saturday, I plain forgot."

For some reason, Jake Wilson looked relieved. He didn't

jump on Jerry for not having what good reporters were supposed to have with them. "We all forget things, Jerry. You remember pretty much what he said, don't you? We don't need all the commas and colons. Wait here. I forgot your Coke."

"Could I have a carton of chocolate milk instead?"

"Right you are. One carton of chocolate milk coming up." Mr. Wilson was humming happily as he left the table.

When he returned, he was smiling. He sat down and leaned across the table toward Jerry. "You know what, Jerry?" he confided. "I have a great idea. I'd like to have you come over to my place on Sunday and put down your interview, what you remember from the three trips, on tape. That way you won't have to worry about keeping notes, and we still won't lose what Mr. Bernard tells you. I'll be right there to jog your memory and ask questions. How does that sound, Jerry? Can your dad spare you for an hour Sunday afternoon?"

When he was coaching him, Dad hadn't thought of a tape recorder. Neither had Jerry. He wondered if it had just now occurred to Jake or if he had been working his way toward this great idea.

"I don't know, Mr. Wilson," he answered at last. "I think I'd have trouble with that. We have one at the house. Mom used to tell me stories when I was little and record them. She didn't have any trouble with it. When Dad tried, it didn't work. He stuttered and stopped and made mistakes. Mom laughed and said he didn't belong in the twentieth century. I guess I don't, either. When Mom left, I intended to send her some tapes about what I was doing each week. It sounded silly when I played it back. I couldn't go on."

Mr. Wilson listened patiently to Jerry's excuses. "It's different, Jerry, when someone else is talking to you, leading you on and asking you things. You're not by yourself. Pretty soon you forget it's even there. I use it all the time in my senior writing class."

Jerry had heard about that class. You couldn't write what you wanted to, kids said. You had to write what Mr. Wilson wanted you to write. Sometimes he made you read what you wrote into the tape recorder and then listen. He laughed at your mistakes.

"I don't think I could, Mr. Wilson."

"Okay, Jerry, you'll just have to write it up for me so I can go over it and edit it for the *Scripture*. We'll print it in installments until old—I mean Mr.—Bernard has finished. When can I have the stuff? Try to do it on Sunday so I'll have it Monday morning. I don't suppose you can type? We can't hold up publication any longer. We're already late."

The moment Jerry wanted to avoid had arrived. "I'm afraid I can't do that, either, Mr. Wilson."

Jake's face turned red. "What is this, Jerry boy? Are you playing games with me again? We're right back where we were on Monday. Are you working for the *Scripture* or not? You have a job to do, Jerry. What about it?"

"I don't know now. I'd like to do the reporting I agreed to do, but—"

"But what, Jerry? You haven't talked to anyone about this, have you?"

"Only my dad—and my mom back in Chicago."

"Jerry, Jerry. What have you done? Your dad's all right, I guess. He never says much about anything. After all, you live with him. But Amy? She'll tell all her new friends how her boy Jerry is spending every Saturday with the great novelist Paul Bernard. I know Amy. She likes to talk. Good-bye to our scoop. We really have to hurry now. Let's not give it away."

"Mom knows this is important, Mr. Wilson. You're wrong. She doesn't talk a lot. She never did."

"Okay, Jerry, if you say so. Do I get the stuff on Monday? The stuff for the first visits plus tomorrow's?"

"I can't do it, Mr. Wilson."

Jake pushed himself back from the table. He stared at Jerry with cold blue eyes. "What the hell is going on, Jerry? Spit it out. I'm not a man people play games with, I can tell you that."

"I know, Mr. Wilson. It's just that I can't do the interview right now."

"For heaven's sake, why? You have to start now or you'll lose it. You should have kept notes after the first meeting. I'm pretty tough on kids who let me down. Your father can't help you. This is high school business."

Jerry had made up his mind as he came to school Friday morning that he wasn't going to hide behind Dad. He would settle the matter directly with Mr. Wilson. "I can't do it because Mr. Bernard said last Saturday that he was going to write the interview for me."

Stunned into silence, Jake leaned back in his chair. At last, he spoke. "Write it for you?"

"Yes, that's what he said."

"When, Jerry?"

"He didn't say, but I think he may be doing it as we go along. That's what Lorna thinks, too."

"For the *Scripture*, Jerry? Paul Bernard is writing for the *Scripture*? I can't believe that."

"I don't think so, either, but maybe. He didn't say."

"For whom, then?"

"I don't really know, Mr. Wilson. I sort of think he's writing it for himself."

"My God, he *is* crazy," Jake exclaimed. "I've never heard of anything as crazy as this. Okay, let me think for a minute." He went to the counter and returned with another cup of coffee.

"Did he say it was confidential, whatever it is he's up to?"

"No, but I think it is, at least for a while—until he decides, I mean."

"But Mr. Bernard didn't say it was off the record. That's what people say when they don't want you to print something. He didn't say that?"

"No."

"Thank the Lord for small favors. We're still in business. I tell you what, Jerry, let's do it this way. If you feel you can't write it down or talk to a tape, you can still talk to me and answer my questions, a sort of interview about the interview. That will let you off the hook. For example, if I were to ask you now, what has Paul Bernard mostly talked about up to this point, what would you say?"

He could answer that question directly, Jerry believed. "Growing up alone. About being a kid by himself on the farm and the river. About his mother and what he did with his father. About the one-room schoolhouse. Stuff like that."

"Anything about what happened to his legs, Jerry?"

"He lost them, I guess. He talks about them, but not about what happened."

"There, you see, something important. People don't know whether he lost them or is just a cripple. That part of his life is a blank. Did you know that, Jerry? Only the outline, that's all we have. All week I've been reading books and articles about Paul Bernard, anything I could lay my hands on in this two-bit town. Until the moment he appeared with his book about the war, there is nothing. Now the farm is gone, made into a marina and summer cottages. His folks are gone, and they had no friends. The teacher is dead. No one has located any schoolmates. They have his record at the hick college, yes, and a professor or two pretend to remember him, but he didn't make any impression there, either. His army record is pretty ordinary. His ex-wife refuses to say a word about him. There's nothing, and he has never written a word about it in a single one of his books. Why? I ask you, Jerry, why?"

"It's private, I guess, Mr. Wilson." Jerry hadn't realized up to now just how private Mr. Bernard's growing up was. It must be important to him for some reason. Lorna told him she had never heard her father talk about the farm and the river. That *was* strange. Mom told Jerry everything about her childhood in Chicago. Dad's life he already knew. Jerry was almost living it again.

Then one day, he thought with awe, a kid—he, Jerry Huffaker—came to the house, and Mr. Bernard opened up. It was weird, and he couldn't begin to understand it. But he did understand that Mr. Bernard wanted that part of his life to stay private. He hadn't said anything like that, but Jerry knew. He wasn't going to repeat any part of what he had heard.

Jake was still talking. "It's unbelievable. You're not old enough to appreciate this, Jerry, but you are sitting on the biggest literary story of the century: Paul Bernard's mysterious past. We'll be famous. I can place this story anywhere in the country. There's no telling how much they'll pay for it. We have to print it. We have a responsibility to the press and the public. That's how a free press works. When can we get together, Sunday?"

Jerry stood up. "I can't do it, Mr. Wilson. I don't think Paul would want me to do it. You see, he's my friend. So is Lorna. Their lives belong to them. You can't betray your friends." Jerry walked through the swinging doors and up the steps. He couldn't be late for math twice this week.

17

IT WAS GOING WELL FOR THE GREAT MAN. THE SNIPPETS
and fragments of his notes were becoming paragraphs and
paragraphs were becoming pages, and before he was aware
of it, the pages were becoming what might pass for chapters.
He'd see about that later, he decided. Perhaps he didn't
need chapters for this. It seemed to be a whole, and it would
be hard to stop and begin somewhere else. Writing an interview with himself would be tricky.

He moved systematically among the memories that thrust
themselves up like a cut-back sumac in the spring. The energy of life from the sun and rain poured into the roots, and
the weedy sprouts shot up in crazy abundance. The sumac
was a worthless, devouring tree, but it was hard, nearly im-
possible, to kill, and for a short moment in the fall its foliage
flared forth like flames.

The image pleased the great man. I am an old stump of a

man, he thought, as legless as the cropped sumac; but he could feel the enormous surge of energy within. His head throbbed with the intensity of his efforts to control the flow of his recollections, to prune them and let them form into a mature and coherent revelation of his beginnings. It must be a coherent and sensible revelation. This was no time to stop writing as people said he wrote, like an angel.

Beyond the wide sliding door, now open, Lorna was sketching on the deck, her camera hanging from the back of her chair. She had been trying to shoot some pictures of Harpo and Mom, but the angle was difficult, and the sea lions were not being cooperative. She wasn't doing any better with her sketch of Harpo peering out of the ocean. She put the pad down and stretched. She walked inside Dad's cave. "If I go down there, they'll slide into the water, won't they?" she asked her father.

"They will, indeed. You will have to be patient—a little bit every day until they are used to your being close. That might work. They recognize us. . . . They just haven't had to put up with our being so close. What are you doing, any-way?" Bernard wanted to know.

"Actually, I've been thinking of putting together a collection of photographs, if it's all right with you." In their sporadic correspondence, her friend Tony had mentioned to Lorna several times that he thought he could place a collection of her photographs. Tony was a literary agent of considerable skill. "But you will have to have some of your father," he demanded, "not just the gulls and cliffs and grass in the wind. I can't sell it without Paul Bernard."

What would Dad say? He hadn't minded when she fussed around his desk with her camera the first couple of years she was in the house. It bothered him so little, she wondered if he was aware of her crouching and leaning and squatting, taking roll after roll of the great man at work.

"Do you mind, Dad?" she asked.

"Mind what?"

"My taking pictures of the cliff and the house and the road and Mrs. Bailey and you and even Jerry? Would you mind if Tony found a publisher for them?"

"Why should I mind, Lorna? I'm no different from Harpo, am I?"

"I guess not. He's just like you. He doesn't want to be bothered, even by Mom."

"I think it's a good idea, Lorna." The great man turned back to his desk. That won't do, he thought, that won't be enough. "How would it be if I wrote a little something to go with them? I could try. You wouldn't have any obligation to use it."

The offer was so unexpected, its acknowledgement of her existence so clear, that Lorna was shaken. I'm going to cry, she told herself. I can't help it. I haven't cried for years, but I'm going to cry now. Tears came to her eyes. She let them come. She ran to the wheelchair and threw her arms around her father and let the tears flow, happy and unashamed.

The great man held her tight, as tight as when as a child she climbed into his legless lap in the apartment. His cheeks were damp with emotion. Damn it, he was crying himself, crying real tears for the first time since old Dr. Manlove called him down to the farm to lay his father in the ground.

He had written about tears since then, but he had not shed them. Life went on in his novels, through joy and, more often, through sadness. He wrote about tradition and survival and the sublime essence of human existence. "You're all I have left, Lorna," he whispered. "How can I deny you?"

Then, "Where's that boy?" he half shouted. "Where's that Huffaker kid? He should have been here by now."

Lorna stood up and pushed the hair from her face. "You don't have to be embarrassed, Dad. A few tears are good for people. They know they are alive. And if you would wear that watch I gave you, Dad, instead of shouting at Mrs. Bailey and me, you'd know it's not time for Jerry to be here."

"Why don't you go and get him, Lorna?" Bernard grumbled. "It's a hard ride up our road."

"He doesn't ride up. He told you that. He pushes his bike up. He wants to. He likes to. It makes him feel independent. Just because you never had a bike . . ."

"Who told you that? I never wanted one. There was no place to ride it."

"There was no place to push an old wheelchair, either, apparently, but you wanted it. What were you going to do with that chair?"

Without thinking, the great man replied, "I was going to hitch Brandy up to it and have him pull me down to the river."

"Brandy? Who was Brandy? Don't tell me you had a pony."

"Of course not, Lorna. Brandy was my dog. I must have told you about Brandy."

Lorna shook her head. "No, you haven't. You have never told *me* anything about your farm and the precious river. You have rambled on to Jerry, and I have listened in, but you weren't talking to me. I have just let you see my tears. Imagine, a thirty-seven-year-old woman crying on her dad's lap! Now you tell me about the dog you were foolish enough to think about hitching to a wheelchair. Let's go out on the deck. You haven't had any fresh air today." She pushed the great man toward the deck.

"I was going out to the cliff later with the Huffaker kid. My legs! It's time to put on my legs," Bernard protested. "Take me inside."

"Your legs can wait. Mrs. Bailey is making a cake for Jerry. I have something for you. Wait here." Lorna ran back inside toward the elevator.

She returned with a brown-and-black object in her hand. She leaned over her father to pull a brown-and-black billed cap squarely onto his head. She stood back to admire him. "It fits you perfectly. I knew it would when I bought it. It will keep the sun from your eyes out here."

"I don't wear hats, Lorna. What is it, anyway?"

"It's a sailfishing hat. I bought it for you in Bimini ten or twelve years ago. I never got around to sending it to you. You wouldn't have worn it."

Bernard fingered the stitching on the front of the cap. "What are these letters, Lorna? You're making a fool of me, aren't you?"

"I'd like to, Dad, but I don't dare. The letters say I LOVE MY DAD. That's what they're supposed to say. Actually, they say RICKS FOR HIRE. Rick must have been a fishing guide. I don't remember. Now, tell me about the dog I never heard of."

Another road had opened up past the signs into the forbidden land. Beyond lay poor, faithful old Brandy. The great man sniffled. Tears for Lorna, sniffles for Brandy. What was happening to him today? He must be on the edge of an emotional collapse, he thought. What could he tell Lorna about Brandy? He was just a big mutt.

He wasn't, of course; he was Brandy. He was never a puppy, it seemed. He was always a full-grown, big, black and brown dog, half Chesapeake Bay retriever, Dad had said; the other half was trouble. A farmer down the road had offered Brandy to his dad, and he had taken Brandy to train him to fetch ducks from the icy river after he shot them. Brandy refused to be trained. He would escape from the shooting blind and run up to the house to Paul. When Dad came up for lunch, wet to his waist from wading in the river to bring the canvasbacks in to shore himself, he would snarl at poor Brandy cowering under the table and promise him he would be a water dog or else.

As he spun the story out to Lorna, it was as clear as if it had happened yesterday. "And Mom,"—Lorna held the word with a steely click of her mind; Dad had a Mom, not a Mama—"who almost never stood up to Dad, would stand up for Brandy. 'You shouldn't shout at the poor dog, Harry. You should have taken a puppy to train. Brandy is a grown dog. He wants to be with Paul, and that's good. The boy has no other friends.' Dad, shivering there in the kitchen, a brace or two of ducks slung over his shoulders, would suddenly laugh. 'That dog is more trouble than retriever.'"

"What a wonderful story," Lorna said. "What did Brandy do to earn his keep?"

"Looked after me. He didn't want to retrieve, but he loved to swim. I'd put my arm around his neck, and Brandy carried me out beyond the crab grass to the channel, where the water was clear and deep. Once in a while he would take me across to the other side, to Haskell's Point. He was a powerful swimmer."

"Did he sleep on your bed?" Lorna asked.

"He was too big. My bed was set real high off the floor. I think it was my grandfather's bed. Brandy would crawl underneath. All night long, he'd heave and grumpus and try to get comfortable. The bed wasn't high enough for him when I was in it. I'd roll over to one side or another so the springs wouldn't sag down on top of him."

"I suppose he walked to school with you," Lorna observed. "That's what dogs did in the stories I read."

"Sometimes he'd want to walk down to the county road, but I chased him home. People stole dogs they thought might be hunting dogs. He waited at the house for me. When I came around the curve in the lane he'd run across the orchard. I'd give him a crust of bread or the baloney out of my sandwich. I can still taste that awful baloney, like a half-dead hot dog. One day baloney, one day blackberry jelly—those were my sandwiches. I was lucky. Lots of kids in the school had only lard sandwiches."

The great man paused to brood on the poverty of the farmers, tenant farmers most of them, living in shacks across the fields from the proper farmhouses. Careworn men and women trying to scrabble a living from the pebbly soil. Batches of kids with rotten teeth and bare feet purple from the cold, taking turns going to school wearing the one or two pairs of shoes they shared. He was lucky. Dad had his own farm. It wasn't any good, but it fed them. And there was the river. That fed them, too. They didn't have to get through the winter on squirrel and rabbit pie or woodchuck stew.

"What happened to your dog, Dad?"

"He got old, the way dogs do. He stayed by the wood-stove most of the time, sleeping. Before I went off into the army—he knew I was leaving; dogs know things like that—he dragged himself out into the woods and died. He didn't want to cause any trouble. I didn't have a dog after that. I sometimes think we should have one here, but . . ."

Mrs. Bailey came through from the kitchen, Jerry Huffaker trailing behind her. "The boy from the *Scripture* is here to interview the great man. Lunch in ten minutes."

18

———— ◆ ————

MR. BERNARD DIDN'T HAVE HIS FAKE LEGS ON. HE WAS impatiently wheeling himself around the big room, rolling from his cave over to Lorna's and back again, shouting to Mrs. Bailey to hurry up with his legs. He wanted to visit Harpo and Mom before the ocean dried up. Lorna hid her nose in a book. Mr. Bernard stopped the chair in front of Jerry, who stood in the middle of the room, between the two caves, waiting.

Looking up at the boy, the great man asked, "You know what, Jerry? Years ago, one day when I was bored with this chair and the gorilla who looked after me before Mrs. Bailey took over, I had the idea of joining the circus. I had visions of being the first legless tumbler in the history of the circus. I could see myself twisting and turning in the air before I came to earth on my hands. I would have been famous. What do you say to that, Jerry?"

"Dad!" Lorna shouted from the white leather sofa. She wasn't reading, after all, Jerry thought. She was listening all the time.

"Dad," she said. "That's crazy talk. What are you teasing Jerry for? Isn't it enough that Mrs. Bailey and I have to put up with you? Don't pay him any attention, Jerry. He's been acting silly all week. Yesterday when Mrs. Bailey and I were strapping on his legs, he said he had half a mind to try to walk down to the beach to have a talk with Harpo and Mom. Can you imagine?"

Mr. Bernard ignored her. "You know what I did, Jerry? I didn't join the circus. I realized just in time I was only making my way into the next book. That's how a writer's mind works; at least, that's how my mind works. It's full of detours and turns and a cul-de-sac or two. That's how I start. Afterward, I go in a straight line."

"What's a cul-de-sac, Mr. Bernard?" Jerry asked.

"Paul! I am a Paul to you, Jeremiah Huffaker, son of Edward and Amy Huffaker. Remember that: Paul am I to you; Jerry are you to me. A cul-de-sac means in French the bottom of the bag. In English it means a blind alley or a dead-end street, something that goes nowhere. Like me."

Mr. Bernard was acting very strange. Was he drunk? Last summer Mom's friend Stu drank too much wine at a little Italian café and acted silly the rest of the evening until Mom told him to go home. Stu minded Mom. He saluted and walked backward to the door with a dumb smile on his face. Later Mom said Stu was a problem sometimes. Jerry looked over to Lorna to see what was going on.

"It's all right, Jerry. Dad's not drunk. A glass of wine a day is all we allow him. It's excitement, I think. He's writing again. We don't know what because he doesn't tell us, but he feels good about it. Other times he's very serious. This time he's having fun. Either way, we have to put up with him." Lorna seemed pleased with the way her father was behaving.

Jerry followed Mr. Bernard across the room to the far corner of the writer's cave. He hadn't been there before. He saw the metal door to the elevator and a door that led, he guessed, into the kitchen. Mr. Bernard was having trouble turning the chair around. Jerry took the back of the wheelchair. "I'll push for a while," he said. "Could you tell me about the circus, please?"

"Thank you, Jerry. My daughter Lorna Melissa is right. I am excited. I am discovering things about myself that are interesting to me, to say the least. Valuable, too. Not to anyone else, but to me, yes. I need these things now. I have run out of other things to write about. I was trying to get back to the circus again, for example. Have you ever been to a circus, Jerry?"

"Once, to the big one that comes to San Francisco every year. I went with Mom and Dad."

"Did you like it?" Paul Bernard asked.

"Not really. I had seen it all before. It was like one of the big shows on television. It didn't seem like the circus to us, at least not what we expected. Mom didn't care. She was glad to be going up to the city. We spent the night in a hotel and walked around the next day. Mom liked that. She made a mistake and told Dad she felt free. That hurt Dad's feelings. It sort of ruined the day."

"He's going to write, Lorna," Mr. Bernard announced. "I told you he was going to write. He can't help it. It's the way he looks at things that is important." Bernard reached up over the back of his chair to squeeze Jerry's hand. "Don't be embarrassed, Jerry, if you are. I can't see your face. Lorna and I talk about you because you are new to us. You are full of surprises, like Harpo and Mom on the days they don't do what we expect them to. Lorna argues that it doesn't mean you will write. It might only mean you'll be an astrologer. But I say she's wrong. What do you say, Jerry?"

"I don't know. I haven't thought about it much. I don't think I'll be a teacher, though. I don't want to tell other people, even kids, what to do. Maybe I'll be a bike rider."

Mrs. Bailey came from the elevator carrying the metal legs and the crutches. "I had to change the strap on one," she said. "There was no call for all that shouting, Paul. Where do you want me to put them on?"

"On my legs, Mrs. Bailey, on my legs. Where else would you put them on?"

"Paul, when are you going to give up on that awful joke? I have enough trouble with these contraptions."

"Jerry will help you, Mrs. Bailey. He's young and strong." Mr. Bernard reached down to pull the trouser legs up past where his knees should have been. Two large, pink stumps protruded over the edge of the chair. Mrs. Bailey knelt down and began to attach one of the steel and plastic frames to the great man's thigh. The stump rested in a plastic cup. That's how it's done, Jerry thought. He had been wondering about that.

"Here, Jerry, you do the left leg," Mrs. Bailey told him. "Lorna usually helps me. You might as well learn, too. I may not be here some Saturday when Paul decides to go for a walk."

Jerry watched Mrs. Bailey closely as she tightened the straps and tested the buckles on the right leg. With her help he slipped the device over Mr. Bernard's left thigh. "Tighter, Jerry," he instructed, "pull the top strap tighter and be sure it's locked. Let's see how they work today."

He waved Mrs. Bailey and Jerry to one side. He took the crutches and stood up. He walked away from the chair, stiffly at first, then easily. He went over to Lorna, bent over, and kissed her cheek.

"How about that, Jerry? I should have joined the circus, after all."

"You could have, I guess. Did you write a book about a circus?"

"In a way, I did. It was a book about a retirement home for old entertainers, circus people, movie people, stage people, vaudeville people. All they had left were their memories. It was their memories I wrote about." Bernard stood in the middle of the room, rocking on his crutches.

"I think it's Dad's best book," Lorna observed. "It's so beautiful it makes you cry. He won three prizes for it, didn't you, Dad? They made it into a play. It was a huge success."

"I didn't see it," the writer muttered absentmindedly.

"Of course you didn't. Why don't you go on and tell Jerry how you came to write it? I'm curious myself."

"I've already told you, Lorna."

"No you haven't, Dad. You only told me you once wanted to be a legless acrobat. I thought it was a joke."

"It was a joke, I reckon. Still, I could see myself bouncing around in the ring, using my body and arms instead of my legs. That must have led me to recall the circus I once saw. Or else it was the circus that led me to want to be a tumbler. You can't always be sure what comes first. Anyway, it was a circus, mine or the real one."

"The big circus?" Jerry asked.

"Good heavens, no. It was an old tent show. There used to be dozens of them roaming the country: circuses, wild west shows, animal shows, carnivals. Dad took me to one down the shore a little after my mother died. One big tent and a smaller tent for the wild animals and freaks. You had to pay extra to get into it. In the big tent, a handful of circus people did everything—sold tickets, performed, did the animal acts, and hawked Crackerjacks and souvenirs when they weren't performing. They were all old and beat-up save for a couple of young girls in tights who pretended to be bareback riders and high-wire artists. I suppose I was disappointed. I had heard of the big show, which never came anywhere near where we lived, and I must have expected the real thing— the stuff you saw, Jerry. Afterward, I wasn't disappointed at all. I remembered the circus smells and the holes in the tent and the worn-out costumes and by magic, you might say, I made a book out of them—along with some other things I made up."

"I'll give you a copy when you leave, Jerry. It's called *Stardust*. What did my grandfather think of the circus, Dad? Do you remember?"

"He must have been more impressed at the time than I was. I doubt he'd ever been to one before. He never talked much, but he probably said something like, 'That was a lot of fun, Paul. Your mother would have liked that.' Whenever anything good happened after she died, he always said Mom would have enjoyed it."

The great man stopped talking. He walked over to the sliding door. With difficulty, he pushed it open. He stood in the opening, rocking back and forth on the crutches again, brow wrinkled, forcing his memory back to the day of the circus. Something was bothering him. He had to find out what it was. Perhaps he could talk it out.

"My dad had an old felt hat," he began. "Brown. At least it had once upon a time been brown. It was stained with sweat and rain and dirt. He wore it everywhere except in the house. My dad was bald—almost bald, anyway—and the hat kept the sun off his head. I never remember him being bald. It's always Dad in his hat I see. It never fell off, even when he bent over to fish his nets or the wind came in suddenly across the bluff into the duck blind. I was just thinking that there was a man in the tent show who had a hat like that. He was one of the clowns—when he wasn't the elephant trainer or selling Crackerjacks. Without his makeup, underneath his old brown hat, he looked like my dad. I must have noticed that and when the time came later, the clown and Dad were all mixed up. That's how it works, Jerry, when you write. It's bits and pieces the tide washes up. To other folks it's just driftwood, maybe one good piece you keep for the living room. To you and me, those pieces are the facts of life. We have to use them."

"The clown was sort of the hero of *Stardust*, Jerry," Lorna said quietly. "Some of the people who write about Dad say he is Dad's finest character. He doesn't have a name. He's just the clown. He's my grandfather. That's who he is."

Bernard looked out to the horizon. The wrinkles on his brow were gone. Jerry didn't know what to say. He waited. Lorna hid her face in her hands.

Mrs. Bailey broke into the silence. "What's going on now? Maybe I should say, 'What's not going on now?' A few minutes ago you were hooting and hollering like I don't know what. What happened?"

Paul and Lorna didn't answer. I guess I'd better, Jerry thought. "Mr. Bernard was remembering the circus, Mrs. Bailey."

"Hmph. Lunch on trays or on the table?"

"We'll come to the table, Mrs. Bailey," Lorna answered. "I think we'll eat together when Jerry is here."

19

THE DAYS GREW SHORTER AS THE CALIFORNIA WINTER, such as it was, set in. When it was raw and damp with the wind from the ocean, Lorna kept the fire burning high in the vast stone fireplace at her end of the room. The deck was piled with the wood Mrs. Bailey's son had trucked up to the house.

Lorna had turned the sofa around to face the fire. Winters were a bad time for her. She had little interest in skiing and less interest in escaping to the city. There was nothing for her there. When she lived in the east, she made her way in the worst months to the islands of the Caribbean to soak up the sun and party from hotel to yacht or terrace or wherever the party was. Sometimes Meredith would fly south with her, doing her duty as a mother, Lorna supposed. That life was behind her now, she realized. Last week at the airport, Meredith, stopping over on her way to New Zealand, had urged Lorna to come along. "Take a break from baby-sitting your father, Lorna," Meredith said. "He'll be there when you get back. South Island is exquisite this time of year."

Lorna had gone to New Zealand with Meredith years ago. It was beautiful. Meredith's roommate from Vassar had married a rich landowner who lived on thousands of acres between the mountains and the sea. Meredith periodically visited Zoë. It had become one of the constants in her life, the visit with Zoë.

"I'll stay where I am, Mother." (Lorna realized, not without bitterness, that Meredith wasn't a Mom or Mama to her, but a Mother.) "I'm not baby-sitting. I'm working on some photographs for Tony. I'm restless every winter, no matter where I am. Anyway, Dad is finally discovering his youth. It's rather nice to be with him now."

Lorna came home and settled in front of the fire.

Paul Bernard would come to visit. He rolled his chair close to the blaze and held out his hands. "The architect told me there was no way in the world of heating this room without destroying it. I didn't used to mind the cold season. Now it's beginning to bother me."

Mrs. Bailey had plugged in an electric heater close to his desk. It didn't do much good. Every time he finished a paragraph, Bernard rolled himself over to Lorna's fireplace. It wasn't only the warmth he sought. It was the company.

"It's like that schoolhouse I went to," he explained to Lorna. "You could never get warm. The teacher, what was her name?"

"Mrs. Maloney, Dad. She was Mrs. Maloney."

"Of course, old Baloney Maloney. She must have weighed over two hundred pounds. Have I told you about her before?"

Lorna nodded. "She drove to school from the next town

over, in a black Ford roadster. When she went home after school she used to take you to the end of the lane in the rumble seat, you and some girl who lived down the road beyond you. The both of you had to clean off the blackboard and beat the erasers."

"Pauline, that was her name. Pauline something or other. She wore black hightop shoes and heavy brown stockings and an old lumber jacket of her father's that smelled of wood smoke. Her father got a job in the shipyard and they left the farm. I sat as far away from her as I could, but it was hard to do in a rumble seat. She was the first girl I ever got close to." Bernard laughed. "I'd rather have walked, but Mrs. Maloney made me get in. 'It will save your shoe leather,' she said."

He looked at Lorna, who was smiling. "You've heard that, too, have you? And the coal bucket beside the iron stove? And the two outhouses out in back? You've heard all of this by now, have you, Lorna?"

Lorna nodded.

"I'm repeating myself, am I? I'm an old bore, a cold old bore. If you talk too much, you're bound to say the same thing twice, sooner or later." Then, anxiously, the great man asked Lorna, "I don't repeat myself to Jerry, do I? I don't want to do that."

"No, Dad. Not to Jerry, just to me. What do you make of that?"

"I make of it that I love you, and I don't care if I bore you or not on a chilly November afternoon when you're not doing anything important that I can see. That's what I make of it, Lorna Melissa." He rolled back to his desk to write another paragraph.

What was he writing over there? Lorna wondered. Was it

the famous interview he had promised Jerry? Was it the diary novel he once told Lorna he would like to write? "Selections from a lifetime diary," he explained. "I'd like to try that some day. It would be difficult to do well, I think." Was it a new novel in which he dared to go far back into his life and recreate it? It had something to do with his growing up, Lorna was certain, but her father gave her no hint of how he was using the fragments he recalled for her in front of the fire.

On good days and on Saturdays, always, good or bad, Paul Bernard strapped on his legs. He and Jerry and sometimes Lorna with her camera went down to the cliff to check up on the sea lions. It was more than an outing now, more than a habit. It was a ritual. Dad would talk sense and nonsense to the boy, testing his stories as he tested his legs. Jerry listened, made a sensible observation, and once or twice teased the great man with a sly remark of his own. Jerry was testing himself, too, Lorna decided.

After that, lunch, and on with the interview, or what Bernard called the interview. "Where was I, Jerry?" he would begin.

"Gee, I don't know, Paul. It's hard to say just where you were. I get confused as I listen to you. When I left, you were talking about some kind of a fish and how you caught them once a year."

"Carp! The High Holidays carp. Good for you, Jerry. I was headed off in another direction this past week. I was going back to school, and I forgot about the fish. Do you know what a carp is, Jerry?"

"No. I've never heard of it."

"It's a big, ugly goldfish with a moustache. They are like cats. They come in all sorts of colors—red, yellow, gold, black—and all mixed up. They graze on the bottoms of ponds and rivers.

"They like grain, and every August my dad would feed them. He scattered buckets of corn and wheat along the shore, and they would come into our cove to feed—the way birds come to a feeding station in a winter storm. Ten days or so before the Jewish holidays, Dad and I would go fishing. There was a call for carp at holiday time."

"You fished with lines?" Jerry asked. The only fishing he had seen was the surf fishermen who stood along the beaches north of the cliffs and cast their lines out into the surf.

"No, no, this was serious fishing. It was for money, which we used to live on or buy something extra with. Dad made nets in the winter, tying squares of cord between the cork line at the top and the lead line at the bottom. He melted the lead sinkers himself. The net was about five feet wide and maybe a hundred and fifty feet long.

"The carp came in at night at high tide to feed on the grain. Dad had his net piled on a rowboat. He'd drop the net in back of the fish from one end of the cove to the other.

"When the tide was low, Dad and I hauled the net in to shore. Dad pulled lines, and I would stomp outside the pocket of the net to keep the carp from burying in the grass to let the lead line slip over them. The carp were as smart as cats, too. Half of them always escaped, over the net or under it. They'd lie in their holes on the bottom and wouldn't move no matter how hard you stomped on them. Sometimes three or four big ones, fifty pounds each, would rush the net at the same time and force an opening. You could see them escape, swimming sideways in the shallow water out to the channel.

"In the end we'd have a net full of flopping, gasping carp. There were always a lot of blue crabs tangled up in the nets.

Dad put them in a bucket for Mom. If there was a pike or a perch, we'd keep that, too, and eat it for lunch. The carp Dad threw into a big wooden box he pulled out to where the water was deep.

"We'd fish two or three nights running. Then Dad would call up Sam the Fish Man, if he hadn't called Dad first. He'd come down to the river in his tank truck. He'd hang his scales to the branch of the red gum tree and they would weigh the fish. It was the same every year. Sam would say the carp were half dead, and he should only pay half price. Dad would drop on purpose the big fish on the beach where about half a pound of sand would stick to them. Sam scraped off the sand and swore at Dad that he was cheating him. After that, they haggled about the price. Finally, they shook hands, and Sam took a big roll of bills from his pocket and counted out the torn and the dirty ones to give to Dad. Before he left, Sam gave me a dollar bill and Dad a big box of shrimp for Mom. He drove down the lane in the sloshing tank truck singing at the top of his voice."

"That was it?" Jerry asked. He couldn't quite see what was so important about catching fish once a year.

The great man sensed the boy's confusion. He understood that Jerry lived in another place in another time. The circumstances in his life came on a color television screen with commercials. You turned them on, you turned them off.

"Look, Jerry," he said, determined to make him understand the rituals that held life together. "Growing up is a series of ceremonies, do you understand? They are how you measure yourself and remember yourself. The rest of it falls between the cracks. You tell me you go home from here Saturday nights, and your father takes you to the Dairy Queen. You expect it now, don't you? It just happens. You don't ask?"

"That's sort of how it happens."

"Did you go to the Dairy Queen when your mother was here? I'd guess not."

"We didn't go. Mom doesn't like soft ice cream."

"But you and your dad go now. And you'll keep on going, probably even if you get tired of soft ice cream. The trip to the Dairy Queen has become a ceremony. It is something special for you and your dad to share. It will become memory. You won't ever forget it. Some day you may write a story called 'The Dairy Queen' about a lucky kid and a good father who was smart enough to know that a trip for soft ice cream helped ease the absence of the boy's mother.

"Well, I went to the river year after year with my father to fish for carp. I didn't give a damn about the fish. It was the ride down to the river in Dad's old truck. It was the September mist rising off the river. It was sloshing around in the water in a pair of Dad's old boots, kicking the fat fish out of their holes because we needed the pennies we got for them. It was my dad sharing part of his life with me and really needing me instead of putting up with me. It was a ceremony. I went home from college to help him fish. I wangled a leave from boot camp at holiday time. Every year I went down from the city in September to stomp around in back of the net. I did that until . . ."

Lorna waited. Dad had come to the door of revelation. Would he open it?

"I think I understand," Jerry said. "It's the way it is when I ride up here. I mean, it's how I feel when I ride up here. I know nothing much is going to happen. We talk to Harpo and Mom, and now we talk around the fire. But it's part of my life, and I won't forget it. I suppose you could call it a ceremony, all right."

20

THE SEPTEMBER ISSUE OF THE *SCRIPTURE* HAD COME OUT late. No one seemed to notice. The October issue had come out on time. Jerry was relieved to see that he wasn't listed among the reporters. In spite of his earlier threats, Jake Wilson paid no attention to Jerry. Once, in the hallway, he stopped and gave Jerry a thoughtful look, then nodded and went on down the hall.

"I hope he's not angry with me," Jerry said to his father the Saturday morning after Thanksgiving. He rolled one of Dad's fresh-made doughnuts in the cinnamon mix. "Sooner or later, I'll end up in one of his classes. Do you think he'll have it in for me?"

"I don't know, Son," his father replied. "Jake is a strange man. The last couple of times we've been together he's avoided me. I suppose he's still unhappy about the Bernard material."

"It wasn't his to use, Dad, even if I had done the interview. It was the school's, wasn't it?"

"Jake probably didn't see it that way," Ted explained. "Your interview would have appeared in the *Scripture*, but Jake would have had the use of it first."

"Maybe he still will. I don't know what Mr. Bernard is up to. He hasn't told Lorna or me directly what he's doing. Lorna says the yellow sheets are piling up on his desk. She used to peek, but not this time. She wants to be surprised. Anyway, she thinks she's heard most of what Paul is doing. They talk a lot these days."

"They didn't before?"

"I guess not. Lorna says he used to be chained to his desk day and night. He grumbled at her if she bothered him."

"His own daughter? That seems sort of odd, Jerry."

"You and Mom didn't talk to me much lots of times, Dad. Sometimes for weeks, it seemed to me."

The chill of reproach ran through Ted. "I'm sorry, Jerry, sorry for your mother and sorry for me. I don't know what happened. We stayed away from each other. We had run out of things to say. We tried not to fight in front of you. We were both angry and ashamed of ourselves, so we kept quiet."

"I wasn't blaming you, Dad. It wasn't that bad for me. Don't worry about it anymore. That's what I told Mom, too. It's really all right. I wasn't the problem you and Mom had. It was different with Paul and Lorna. It's complicated with them."

"They were apart for a long time, Jerry, you said. That must have made a difference."

"Probably. Lorna feels she never had a home. She says she expected more from her father when she decided to come out here to live with him. But he had lived alone so long, he couldn't get used to her, and he was writing so hard he couldn't make time for her. It wasn't that he didn't love her or not want her around. She had to look after herself and felt left out. Paul's been having a tough time writing. It hasn't been easy for him. She thinks he's hung up on his accident."

"With his legs?" Ted asked.

"Lorna says it wasn't the loss of his legs. That hasn't bothered him too much. It was how he lost them, however that was, that he can't talk about. It's all mixed up, and now he's trying to straighten it out."

"That's what psychiatrists and counselors are for, Jerry. It's odd he never used one, or did he? Did Lorna say?"

"Lorna doesn't think so. She can't see Paul confessing to anyone, she says. Up to now he's needed the secret. It kept him writing. I don't really understand what she's talking about."

Paul Bernard has had to come to terms with himself, Ted thought, and he's using my son as his sounding board. It didn't seem to be bothering Jerry. He wasn't curious about Bernard's mysterious past. He's getting something now from Bernard and Lorna that Amy and I couldn't provide. It was their open acceptance of him, he supposed, an acceptance of Jerry for what he was, not what he was to them. What a strange relationship. What would Jerry make of it when he was an adult? Amy would understand these things better than he did. Jerry would talk to her after Christmas. It was too bad Amy wasn't here now. Jerry needed her. And so do I, Ted realized one more time.

Was Bernard right? Was Jerry to be a writer? Somehow that didn't fit Ted's understanding of his son. He knew enough of Bernard by now to sense that his greatness came from a lonely anguish. Nothing like this had happened to Jerry. He was pretty sure that the separation had caused no great shock. Jerry accepted things as they came to him. He thought about them and generally made sense out of them for himself. Like that silly episode with Jake Wilson. Later, maybe, Jerry would have trouble. He and Amy would have to watch and wait and see.

"It's about time for you to leave, isn't it, Jerry?"

"Okay, Dad. I'll get ready. What shall I tell Lorna about Christmas?"

"They really want us there for Christmas dinner?"

"That's what Lorna said. Just for dinner. No presents or anything. She says she's been deprived of an old-fashioned Christmas all of her life, and she's not going to be deprived any longer. She's already ordered a big tree. Like it or not, her father is going to be a human being one day a year. She showed me a big Christmas stocking she had for him. 'I'm stuffing it with everything I've ever bought him and never dared give him because I was afraid my feelings would be hurt when he didn't pay attention,' she told me."

"You can tell her we'll be there, Jerry. We can open our own presents in the morning. You'll open your mother's in Chicago. You'll have three Christmases this year. Think of that!"

Jerry slipped the bicycle clips over his ankles and zipped his jacket. "Okay, Dad, I'm off. I'll see you."

"If you want me to pick you up, call me. I'll be home all afternoon. You don't have to be a bother to Lorna."

"Maybe I'll leave before it's dark. If I don't, Lorna always says bringing me back gives her something to do."

Jerry looked at his watch when he came to Bernard's road.

He had chopped four minutes off his best time. A strong wind had been in back of him since he turned south from Smithville. He felt good about the new record. He slipped off the seat to push the bike up the hill.

Halfway to the house he heard a car behind him. Thinking it was probably Mrs. Bailey, he pushed the bike to the side of the road as he turned to greet her.

It wasn't Mrs. Bailey. It was Jake Wilson in his sporty little red convertible. He had on driving gloves and a checkered cap. "Hi, Jerry," he said. "Give you a lift?"

Jerry shook his head. What a stupid question. There was no room for his bike in Mr. Wilson's car. He continued up the hill. Mr. Wilson followed him.

Jerry stopped. "Did you want to talk to me, Mr. Wilson?"

"Nope," Jake said. "It's no good talking to you. I want to talk to the great man himself. I was hoping you would introduce me. I figured out I would have to do the interview myself, since you weren't being cooperative, Jerry boy."

He didn't have any answer to that. Jerry leaned forward and went on pushing. Jake followed behind.

At the house, Jake parked his car in back of Mrs. Bailey's old Plymouth. He stood in back of Jerry as he knocked at the door to the kitchen. "You have to use the back door, do you, Jerry?" he whispered.

"Come on in, Jerry."

Jerry went in, Mr. Wilson a step behind. Lorna was at the stove. "How are you this morning, Jerry?" She turned to see Jake Wilson. "Oh, is this your dad, Jerry?"

"No. I'm not Jerry's dad. You must be Lorna, is that right? I'm pleased to meet you."

"Who are you?" Lorna asked pleasantly. "Do you know him, Jerry?"

"I'm Jake Wilson, Lorna. I have a sort of interest in Jerry, you might say. I'm his faculty advisor for the school newspaper."

"I didn't ask him," Jerry explained. "He followed me up the road."

Jake smiled. "Jerry has been avoiding me recently. It's a personal problem. I thought it would be a good idea to discuss it with your father. We like to keep track of our students."

Lorna smiled again, more of a frosty smile now than a friendly one. "I think I understand, Mr. Wilson."

"I'm glad you do, Lorna. Jerry must have told you who I was."

"Not really. He may have mentioned you once."

"He did tell you he came up to interview your father for the high school paper."

"He told me that, and he told my father. He just didn't talk about you. Isn't that right, Jerry?"

Jerry nodded. He could see that Jake was determined to talk to Mr. Bernard. He couldn't stop him. He decided that Lorna couldn't, either.

"You see, Lorna," Mr. Wilson went on, "our boy Jerry Huffaker here had an assignment I gave him when the Nobel Prize was announced. After that, Jerry kept the interview for himself. He refused to give it to our paper. I decided it was time to find out what the trouble was, since Jerry couldn't explain himself. He represents the paper, and we want his material. Perhaps I could explain all this to your father."

"We didn't doubt for a minute that he was a reporter for the *Scripture*, Mr. Wilson. There been no confusion."

"Perhaps not, Lorna, but I couldn't really believe him when he told me your father was writing the interview. You will admit that *does* sound unusual. If I could talk to your father, I'm sure we can straighten it all out."

"You may be right, Mr. Wilson, you may be right. My father doesn't generally receive strangers. He gave an interview to Jerry because Jerry was *my* friend. He and I discovered we had interests in common, like sea lions. I'll be right back."

"What's she talking about, Jerry boy?" Mr. Wilson asked. "How did you meet Lorna Bernard? You haven't been leveling with me, Jerry. It's a good thing I came up here."

Lorna returned before Jerry had to answer. "Come along, Mr. Wilson." She led him through the door into the big room. "He's at his desk over there. You can introduce yourself."

Paul Bernard pushed himself back from his desk as Jake Wilson approached. "I am Paul Bernard. You have something to say to me?" He did not take the hand Jake Wilson offered. "I can't ask you to sit down. I have the only chair in this part of the room, and you can see that I can't let you have it."

The great man listened impassively as Jake Wilson told him his business. When he had finished, Bernard spoke. "As I understand it, you don't believe what your reporter Jeremiah Huffaker told you, and you have come to take care of the interview yourself for the school newspaper. You have a distrusting nature, Mr. Wilson. Jerry told you I offered to write the interview, or something like it, for him. That is so. He has felt obliged apparently to honor a trust between himself and his source. That strikes me as a professional attitude. I must honor my half of that trust, sir. I am unable to discuss the matter further." The great man turned back to his desk.

"But," Jake Wilson sputtered. "You have no right to—"

"I have every right, sir. The sign at the bottom of my road gives me the right. You are trespassing. You are here in violation of *my* rights. I ask you to leave. I have work to do."

21

"JAKE WENT AWAY AND THAT WAS IT?" AMY ASKED. "HE must have been crushed. Jake Wilson has a very large ego," she explained to Stu, who had left the empty computer screen to listen.

"He came out of the big room. He went out the door and drove away. He didn't say a word to Lorna or me. He hasn't come near me since then. Dad says he's thinking about what to do next. The worst thing is I have to take American literature with him next semester."

"Dad can talk to the principal, Jerry," Amy said.

"He doesn't think that would be right. I sort of agree. Mr. Wilson hasn't done anything to me. If I keep my work up, he can't flunk me. He'll just try to embarrass me or something, the way he does to other kids who get on his bad side."

Stu went back to the computer and hunched forward. He

pushed a couple of buttons. Nothing much happened. "Stu is trying to start his book," Amy said. "Why don't we go uptown and have lunch at Marshall Field's? I want to buy your father a Christmas present for you to take back. And you'll need boots to keep your feet dry in this awful sludge. This kind of weather makes me think I should have stayed where I was."

Stu grunted. He pushed another button.

"Stu has been trying to write that book for a year," Jerry's mother confessed at lunch. "If he doesn't publish some things pretty soon, the university will fire him. Stu's like your friend Mr. Bernard. He has writer's block." She sighed. "I wish he had his own computer. He's beginning to depress me."

"Paul is writing like crazy now, Lorna says. Some Saturdays we only talk for a little while. You can see he wants to get back to his desk. Lorna says I shouldn't be disappointed if some Saturdays he won't have any time at all."

"Does that bother you, Jerry? I mean, you ride all the way up there to see him."

"I don't go just to talk to Paul, Mom. In the first place, it's a great ride on my bicycle. I like being with Lorna and Mrs. Bailey. And Harpo and Mom, I always spend time with them. It's good for me. I don't have too many friends at high school yet. Every Saturday right after we go to the Dairy Queen, Dad and I talk about my trip to the Bernards'."

Jerry went on to explain to Amy what the great man had said about ceremonies. "He said ceremonies are what hold people together these days until something new comes along to do the job. He says everything else has worn out. Do you understand?"

"I think so, Jerry. People can't live the way they used to when he was growing up. They're pushed around by forces they can't control. You and Dad are learning a lot from Mr. Bernard, aren't you? I envy you."

Jerry noticed that his mother was serious now, not sarcastic the way she sometimes was when she was talking about herself. "I didn't make a mistake when I walked out, Jerry. You and I know that. So does Dad, I hope. I was ready to explode. I wasn't able to do anything for myself. I had housewife's block, you might say. I just had to find some things out for myself and some things about myself. I *had* to go to work. I was trained to have a professional career. I only worked the first year we were married, while Dad finished his M.A. And then that silly personnel job I took in San Jose, that lasted exactly six weeks. The old Datsun and I quit at the same time. Now I'm finding things out, but I'm not sure I'm happy with them. I guess that's what usually happens. Don't you want your salad?"

Jerry shook his head. "I'll have dessert, though."

"Fine. I'll take your salad and order you a dessert. What do you want?"

"Blueberry pie. Lorna makes it once in a while. She's learning to cook from Mrs. Bailey."

Amy waved to the waitress. My son has gone off and found himself another mother, she thought. And a grandfather. She wondered where that left her. Had she become a stepmother? It was time, she realized, to be honest with Jerry and herself.

"I've made some important decisions about my life, Jerry, in the last year."

"I forgot to ask for vanilla ice cream on my pie," Jerry said. "That's what Lorna says."

"What? That you should have ice cream on her blueberry pie?"

"No, that she's making decisions now about her life."

"What does she mean? Do you know, Jerry?"

"She means that she never took charge of her life before. She was wasting herself in the city. She didn't like what she was doing. She said she didn't have any roots. The first really important thing she did was to dump herself down with her father, she said. It gave her time to think. Now, she's doing a book of photographs and sketches. She's going to send you some of me when she gets some she likes. I gave her your address."

"You may have to give her another one. I may move to a smaller place to get rid of Stu in my living room. I don't think I'll be able to put up with him much longer. Maybe I'll get a job somewhere else."

"Where would you go, Mom?" he asked.

"I don't know. That's what I wanted to talk to you about. I promised to give the agency two years. That will be up in the spring. Then, well, I don't know. I'm not doing anybody much good in my job. I can't solve other people's problems by myself. They have to help, too, so I can help them. That's not what's happening. My cases rely on me to look after them, like I came to rely on Dad to keep me going and then got angry when he took over."

"Dad says he wished you had really fought for what you wanted way back when you weren't happy," Jerry told her.

"He said that? He actually said that? I can't believe it. He never said that to me."

"I think he was afraid to. He might not have liked what you said back to him. When we talk about Mr. Bernard, Dad says he can relate to what's going on between Lorna and Paul."

They didn't speak for a while. Amy lit a cigarette as she drank her coffee. She noted Jerry's disapproval. "The first of the year I'm giving them up, Jerry. Even Stu can't put up with them. Poor old Stu. What do you think of him?"

"Not much, I guess," Jerry replied. "It's like waiting for Harpo or Mom to do something different. After a while at least they go into the water. Stu just sits there."

"He's having problems, and I can't help him. Did you know Stu and Dad and I were all students at the university together? Stu stuck around when we went off. He's glued to where he's at now."

Amy lit another cigarette. She put it out almost at once. Why wait? she thought. She crumpled up the half-full pack and put it on the salad plate. And why wait with Jerry, either? She might as well find out if Ted still had room for her.

"Tell me, Jerry, how would it be for you if I talked to Dad about getting together again? Would that be all right with you?"

Jerry thought this might be what Mom was leading up to. "Dad hasn't changed much, Mom, and neither has Santa Juana. I probably haven't, either."

"People always change when something bad happens. I think your dad has, and I know I have. And you're changing every day, Jerry. This thing with the Bernards has made you both think differently. I can see that."

I'm not going to beg, Amy told herself. It might not work out the next time, either. But we could try. She knew enough now to do things for herself. The director at the agency said there were opportunities opening up for social workers to be consultants. Maybe she could have her career *and* her family. Ted had certainly changed, too. He had never talked with Jerry the way he did now. He was trying hard to understand what was happening to his son as he grew up. She and Ted could build on something like that, she was certain.

"He loves you, Mom. I know that. He's always saying so, not just to make me feel good. He says it halfway to himself. But he doesn't want to be hurt again, either. It was awful when you left. Dad couldn't take it again."

"It won't happen again, Jerry. Maybe it will never happen. I only want to start talking to him about it." Amy had a sudden suspicion, a sudden jealous suspicion. "How does he get along with Lorna Bernard? You two went up there for Christmas dinner."

"That's the first time he ever saw her, except to say thank you when she brings me home. It was nice, but all we did was sit around the table listening to Paul tell us about his Christmas years on the farm. 'The ghosts of my Christmas past,' Paul called them."

"No presents?"

"It wasn't a present time for us. Lorna wanted to prepare a Christmas dinner to celebrate with her father. It was nice."

Relieved, Amy put on her coat. "Let's go find you some boots. Who knows? It may snow in California some day. And not a word to Dad about our talk. Agreed?"

"Agreed," Jerry replied. He put his hand behind his back and crossed his fingers.

22

HER FATHER'S HABITS WERE CHANGING, LORNA NOTICED. She confided to Jerry, "He's always done everything that mattered to him for himself. Things that didn't matter he left for Mrs. Bailey or me to do—like his mail or his legs or his meals, things he didn't care one way or another about because they got in the way of his writing. Now—would you believe it, Jerry?—he has decided to take up cooking. He pushes his chair over to the fire and reads recipe books and makes lists of groceries for Mrs. Bailey to buy at the market."

"I bet Mrs. Bailey doesn't think much of that," Jerry observed. She didn't even like Lorna puttering around in her kitchen at lunchtime. She put up with it, but she didn't like it.

"That's what one would think. But she helps him. He's learned where everything is. He stumps around from the stove to the sink to the refrigerator, sometimes without his crutches.

"That's another thing. This week he decided to put the legs on himself. We're afraid he won't get them on tight enough and will fall. At least he lets us inspect the job before he takes off."

Lorna and Jerry were huddled at the top of the cliff waiting for the sea lions to roll into the water or bark or show some signs of life. "Some days the lazy things don't even open their eyes," Lorna complained. "I went down to Smithville yesterday to mail Tony some photographs. I passed the fishmarket and stopped to buy two fresh fish. I tossed them down to the beach. Dad said he used to feed them. No response at all. I think the tide carried the fish out. It's chilly out here, Jerry. Let's go sit by the fire and wait for the great man to finish his paragraph."

"You still don't know what he's writing?" Jerry asked.

"Oh, I know all right. At least, I think I know. It's the interview. It has to be. But there's another thing, Jerry. While you were gone, he decided he had to have pads of white paper, just like the yellow pads but *white*, to write on.

"'Dad,' I said, 'You have a closet full of yellow pads in your study.' 'Yes,' he told me, 'but I want some white ones, too.' I had a feeling if I hadn't gone straight to town to get them, he'd have gone out to the car himself and taken off for Smithville."

"Does Paul drive?" Jerry asked with surprise. He had never thought of him doing that.

"He did for a while. I mean, he didn't, but he could. It was part of his therapy. The gorilla he talks about taught him. He had a car with special controls. Mrs. Bailey said when she came it was sitting in the garage rusting in the salt air. He told her to get rid of it one day; he had better things to do than drive around."

Jerry was interested in Mr. Bernard's strange behavior. He could see him putting his legs on, but messing around in the kitchen or taking off in a car down the crooked hill, that didn't figure. Even the white pads seemed a little strange. Jerry was used to seeing the desk covered with sheets of lined yellow pages, what was finished in neat piles along the edge and everything else scattered all over the desk. "What did Paul do with the white paper?" he asked Lorna.

"I kept track of that, I can tell you," she replied. "He started to write on it at once. Now, part of the time he writes on his yellow pads, the same as always, and other times on the white pads. The white pages he puts in an old typing box. He keeps the lid on, so I'll know it's private."

"He's working on something else, isn't he?" Jerry asked.

"I guess that's what it is," Lorna said, "unless he's putting together recipes for a cookbook. That wouldn't surprise me, either."

No sooner had Jerry and Lorna come in the room to stand by the fire than the great man pulled himself out of his chair and made his way over to Lorna's cave. It seemed to Jerry he used the crutches only for balance, not support. He faced Jerry squarely, staring intently into the boy's face.

"You look pretty well adjusted to me, Jerry Huffaker," he grumbled. "Don't you miss your mother?"

Jerry was stunned. Mr. Bernard had never before asked a really personal question. And he didn't pry into Mr. Bernard's personal life. If Mr. Bernard wanted to tell him, he listened, but he never asked questions and almost never made any comments. Paul was serious now, that was clear. He wasn't teasing. Was this what Lorna was talking about when she said she didn't know what to expect next from her father?

"I miss her, that's for sure," he answered slowly, "but I just saw her in Chicago."

"But you don't live with her, you live with your father up the road a piece in Santa Juana. Why is that, Jerry Huffaker?"

It was an attack. His friend Paul was changing the rules. It was Paul Bernard who was supposed to be interviewed, not Jerry. "Well," he began, "Mom sort of wanted to make it by herself, and I would have been in the way. And I wanted to stay where I grew up. I was used to it. And . . ." Jerry paused.

"And what?" the great man demanded.

"Dad. Stop it this minute," Lorna interrupted. She was angry, very angry. Jerry had never heard her talk to her father so harshly.

Paul Bernard rocked back and forth on his crutches. "Let him answer, Lorna. I have to know. And what, Jerry?"

"And Dad needed me, I guess. He didn't say so, but I knew it. I just did."

Bernard relaxed. He looked down at Jerry, a crooked smile on his face, and reached out to squeeze his shoulder. "I had to know, Jerry. It was none of my business, but I had to know. I told Lorna the first day you showed up, I told her you were your dad's boy. Do you remember, Lorna?"

Lorna didn't. She was pretty sure her father hadn't said anything of the kind. Since it seemed to matter so much to him, she replied, "I'm not sure, Dad. You probably did."

"Are you certain your father needed you, Jerry?" the great man asked next.

It was easy now for Jerry to respond. What Paul asked was

a question, not a demand. He wasn't betraying Dad. His father hadn't made any secret of how deeply Amy's departure affected him.

"Yes. He was lonely. Mom and Dad had their differences, but she was always there. He missed her. Maybe he just missed having someone around, but I think he missed her. Dad collapsed. I had to fill in for a while."

"He didn't have anyone else?" Paul asked.

"No one close. Dad doesn't have many good friends. He keeps to himself. With Mom gone, he only had me. He's all right now. He and Mom are talking to each other. I think Mom wants to come back home."

"That's great," Lorna said. "When?"

"I'm not sure. In a while, maybe. She has to have something to do or it won't work."

"Like me, isn't that right, Dad?" Lorna said.

Paul Bernard didn't answer. It seemed that he didn't hear. He was putting things together in his memory, fitting the pieces of his childhood puzzle into a picture he could recognize.

"It always hurt when I thought about Mom," he told Lorna and Jerry. "She died before I could explain and make it right. I couldn't let myself think about it anymore. I was always Dad's boy. He didn't need me until Mom died, but he let me tag along when he'd rather have been by himself. It was Mom who needed me, because she didn't have much of Dad. He was always in the fields or at the river or out in the barn. But Mom didn't get much of me, either. As soon as I got home from school, I'd run off to find Dad. The summers I spent at the river with Dad or Brandy.

"Then she was gone and when she wasn't there, Dad and I found out how much we missed her and needed her. I could never explain that to myself. Later I could have, I suppose, but I didn't want to. I must have tried to make it up to Dad. Is that how it was for you, Jerry?"

"It was worse for you, Paul. Mom wasn't dead, she was just gone. And we lived in a town and had places to go to."

"But you and your father, you were a team, weren't you? You kept track of each other. And you were careful with each other, right? Isn't that how it was, Jerry? You didn't want to lose each other."

Jerry thought back over the eighteen months of Mom's absence. Paul was right; that's how it was. He and Dad were very careful and polite with each other, like they were afraid they were holding something precious together that they couldn't drop and break. How did Mr. Bernard know these things?

"Yes, that's how it was."

"But my mother was gone for good, and we were alone on a worn-out farm and I had to grow up, and I had to look after Dad maybe more than he had to look after me, like you with your father, Jerry. But with a difference. Dad started to drink, and he didn't stop. He wasn't a proper drunk, mind you, but he drank and the more he drank the less he spoke. I didn't know what to do with that. I took to living inside myself, too. Dad, he needed me more than ever, but he couldn't bring himself to say so. It wasn't Mom's death altogether. It was the failure of his life on the farm. Nothing worked out. He withdrew into some crazy dreams he got out of the bottle. Still, he needed me. I knew it then and I've known it every day since then. And I went away to college and the army and left him. I didn't have to go, but I did."

Again Lorna waited. Her father had returned to the fateful door that was locked. He stood there in front of it, chin rest-

ing on his chest, rocking on his crutches, frowning to himself.

Once again, he turned away. "It's back to work. I was
going to fix lunch for you, Jerry. Mrs. Bailey is teaching me
to cook. But not today. I have things to put on paper. Maybe
next Saturday. I'll have a sandwich, please, Lorna."

23

———◆———

"THIS IS A GOOD READING LIST JAKE GAVE YOU," DAD SAID. "Let's see: *Huckleberry Finn, The Red Badge of Courage, The Red Pony, Catcher in the Rye,* and *Stardust.* We have them all in my study, except for *Stardust.*"

"Lorna has a copy I can have. She said it didn't seem to go with the other books. It's not a good book for high school kids, according to her."

"Why don't we read it together, Jerry? We can talk it over before you discuss it in class. I have an idea Jake Wilson is going to ask you about it. It's not beyond him to have put *Stardust* on the reading list to try to catch you in some way. What he did at the Bernards' was inexcusable. Your mother still thinks I should have gone to the principal about that. She said it was harassment."

Jerry listened more attentively. Dad was talking about Mom again. Once or twice a week, when he had gone to bed, Jerry heard Dad talking seriously on the phone. He

· 134 ·

came down the hall from his room one night to listen. It seemed as though they were talking about nothing in particular, but he did hear Dad say, "Well, Amy, you're the one who will have to decide. You know how I feel—the same as I've always felt." Jerry crept back down the hall, his heart beating a little faster. Maybe, just maybe. He recited a little prayer he had learned in Sunday school to use whenever you wanted something real bad.

Later, Dad would say, "I talked to your mom last night. She's in pretty good spirits these days," or "Your mom sends you her love, Jerry," or "Things aren't going so well for Mom on her job." What Dad didn't say was "Your mom and I talked about getting together," or "Mom thinks it's time to come back," or "I told Mom we needed her as much as ever," or, best of all, "I told Amy we loved her and to please come back as soon as possible."

Lorna said she thought it would work out. She had spread her photographs, and some sketches of Paul that he had never seen, all over the floor of her cave. She stood over them peering down. From time to time she selected one and put it in a pile. She was sending those to Tony. "The others, I don't know. I think I'll make my own private album and keep adding to it."

There were two of Jerry and Paul. The first was the boy and the great man at the cliff, leaning into the wind. Jerry was looking down at Harpo and Mom, Paul gazing into the horizon. He had his left hand on Jerry's shoulder for support. The other was in the middle of the big room, close to the glass. Jerry was saying something, and Paul was smiling his crooked smile as he listened.

"I matted these two and sent them to your mother in Chicago. Is the address you gave me still good? I forgot to ask."

"It must be. She hasn't said any more to me about moving. Dad calls her up all the time now—well, not all the time exactly, but about twice a week regularly. They're getting reacquainted, Dad says. He doesn't say much else. I think he's afraid he'll jinx it if he talks too much—like Paul says, you can ruin things if you worry about them too much."

"She'll be home again, Jerry," Lorna said. "She has too much of her life here. If she hadn't loved you both, she wouldn't have stuck it out as long as she did. I felt the same way here with Dad, lost and out of place, for the longest time. I wanted to be here and at the same time I wanted to be somewhere else doing something useful.

"I was happy and I was unhappy. There wasn't much I could do for Dad. Mrs. Bailey took care of that. About the time you came up the hill with your bike, I got out my camera and sketching stuff. I remember that when I saw you and Dad face to face I knew it was something I might not ever see again—the man and the boy, the man in the boy, and the boy in the man—and I had to put it down, not in words because, like you, I'm not much of a writer, but with the tools I had. I've been busy and happy ever since. Tony says the photographs are great, and Dad has promised to write something about himself to go with them. Maybe that's what he's keeping in the box at his desk."

Lorna separated the sketches from the photographs. She lined them up against the wall. "I'm not certain about these. What do you think, Jerry? Tony says I'm a better photographer than an artist. He's right, but when you do something with your bare hands, not the camera, you're closer to it somehow and it's more of what you meant to say."

Jerry studied the sketches. They were all of the great man at his desk. They didn't seem to be what Paul was as much as in the photographs. Except for one. Paul was leaning back in his chair, his eyes turned to the ceiling. He was rubbing his chin. Lorna had put in all the wrinkles and the furrows in his brow. He was tired and, in a way, tormented. Jerry put his toe toward the drawing: "I like that one."

Lorna picked the drawing up. "That was one day right after you came. He was still having trouble with his writing. He was wearing out from what he had been doing day after day, year after year, with never a break. Like my grand-father, I suppose, on that useless farm." Lorna hesitated. "Do you want it, Jerry? I'll mat it for you."

Jerry nodded. There was something haunting in Paul's ex-pression that made him want to cry. For a moment, Mr. Bernard was helpless. It was the way Dad looked right after Mom left, saddened, helpless, and a little scared. "Yes, please," he said at last. "I'd like to have it if you don't want it."

"It's yours." Lorna laid the sketch on the table in back of the sofa. "Say," she said, "I've been meaning to ask. What-ever happened to that teacher who came up here before Christmas, Mr. Watson or something? You have him for a course, you said."

"Mr. Wilson, Jake Wilson. He's okay, I suppose. He hasn't bothered me since then."

Which was more or less true. Jake had torn his composi-tions to shreds, but he hadn't bothered Jerry about Paul Ber-nard. Mr. Wilson was someone he didn't want to talk about except with Dad. Jerry was still embarrassed about Jake's appearance at the Bernard house. Paul and Lorna appeared to have forgotten about it. At least they never mentioned it, and Jerry had brought it up only when he asked if he could borrow a copy of *Stardust* for Jake's course.

"Oh, that man," Lorna had said and went up to Paul's

study where, she reported, there were ten or twelve copies of the novel. She came back by way of Paul's desk. She said something to him. He took the book and wrote in the front. "Here you are, Jerry," Lorna said. "It's yours to keep."

In the front, Paul had written, "For Jerry Huffaker and his dad. You will both understand this one—Paul."

Dad had read *Stardust* first, slowly, carefully, the way he read everything, even the daily paper, which used to upset Mom because she always wanted the section Dad hadn't finished reading.

"I've never read anything like it, Jerry," his father announced. "He must be the best there is, like everyone says. You say the clown is Mr. Bernard's father?"

"Not his father exactly. It's the hat the clown always wears, even when he's in the retirement home. He wore it all his life in the circus. It's Paul's father's hat. Paul isn't certain whether the clown is his father or not. But he must look like him. If the hat's the same, the face must be, too."

Once more Ted was struck by his son's perceptions. Such a thought would never have occurred to him. Jerry was right. You couldn't separate a hat from the face underneath. They went together.

"Is that what the master said?" he teased. As he grew closer to his son, he allowed himself to tease Jerry a little bit. He had never done that before. Like the hat on the face, it never occurred to him.

"No. Paul never talks about what he's written, just how he came to write it. Lorna talks, but not Mr. Bernard. He doesn't read reviews, and he doesn't read the books people write about him. That makes Lorna a little angry. She tells him he ought to realize how great he is to the people who know."

"And what does Paul say to that?" Ted asked.

"He laughs. He says he already knows how great he is, and if he read everything they wrote about him, he might end up not being so great."

"Is he right, Jerry?"

"I think so. If I listened to Mr. Wilson tell me how awful my first three papers were, I'd probably drop out of school. Two D's and an F and about ten pages of nasty comments. I see what the other kids write, the papers Mr. Wilson gives an A or B to. My papers are just as good."

"They're better, I'm sure. Amy and I discussed what we should do. We'll save the papers. If Jake keeps this up, and it looks as though he'll fail you, I'll take them to Phil Tassone. He's head of the English department. If we have to, I'll go to the principal. Your mom thinks Jake is trying to soften you up to write something important on the *Stardust* paper. She may be right."

"He'll be disappointed. I haven't even started. He can give me an honest F on that one. Can we go to the Dairy Queen early?" Jerry asked. "I'll start on it tonight."

"What seems to be the problem? I think you know what the book is about. It's reliving your life through your memories."

"That's not the problem, Dad. It's doing this paper the way I've done the others—I mean, without letting on that I know how Mr. Bernard worked his way into the book. That's what Jake is waiting for. Then he'll pounce. He's trying to trap me. That sounds sick, but I'm certain that's what he's up to."

"It's not sick, Jerry. It's Jake Wilson who is being irrational. All you can do is be objective. Stick to the novel and what it says and what you think of it. Just stick to the book. Get your jacket. We'll go now. I sometimes wonder why they keep the Dairy Queen open in the winter. There's never anyone there Saturday nights."

24

BY MIDNIGHT JERRY HAD THE FIRST PARAGRAPH OF HIS
paper written. It wasn't anything to get excited about, but
there wasn't anything wrong with it, either. He had found
some facts about *Stardust* in one of Dad's books. He supposed they were correct. He read the paragraph over one
more time before he turned out the light on his desk and
crawled into bed.

> Seventeen years ago Paul Bernard's novel *Stardust* was
> published. It was a great success and went through
> many printings. *Stardust* won three major prizes for the
> best novel of the year. It was made into a play which
> ran in New York for eighteen months. Mr. Bernard re-
> fused to sell the rights for making a film out of *Stardust*.

In bed Jerry thought about the rest of the paper. Mr.
Wilson had insisted that it be three pages long. So far he had

written less than half a page. He couldn't use up more than two and a half pages telling the story, because there wasn't that much of a story to tell. He remembered that Lorna had told him that the reviewers said it was Mr. Bernard's greatest work.

Jerry crawled out of bed. If he had the first sentence of the next paragraph down, it would be easier to keep on going in the morning. His pencil had fallen to the floor. He picked it up and wrote on the yellow pad Dad had bought him for good luck, "Many people think *Stardust* is Paul Bernard's"—he didn't want to say "great" again, because Mr. Wilson hated seeing the same word all the time—"most important novel." He studied the sentence. Satisfied, he turned out the light again. That will do it, he told himself; that will get me started in the morning. I can find some more remarks like that and tell the story on the last page and a half. Three pages were a lot. He wondered what the other kids would do.

What some of the other kids did was stay home. Jerry counted only eleven of the sixteen kids on hand Monday at ten o'clock. All the girls were there, but five boys were absent, leaving only George Klein, Tim Mendoza, and Jerry. He felt alone in the back row. Mark and Billy, who sat on either side of him, had taken the day off. In his bones Jerry could feel that it was going to be a bad day. He put the copy of *Stardust* in the middle of his desk, the composition folded in half and tucked securely in the book.

Mr. Wilson came in, followed by a stranger. Jake had on a bow tie and a suit. That was a bad sign. Usually he wore a beat-up corduroy jacket and no tie at all. The stranger was a fat, little old man who was getting bald. He looked about as nervous as Jerry felt.

"This is Will Purvis," Jake announced. "He's a friend of mine from San Francisco who writes about modern American literature for newspapers and magazines. I have persuaded him to join us. He is writing a book of his own about the man whose novel we are reading, Paul Bernard. I thought he might be interested in what the class had to say. Later in the hour he may have some questions. Tomorrow he will talk to you about Bernard."

The fat little stranger made his way to the back of the room to sit in Billy's seat. He gave Jerry a quick smile.

"I think today, instead of my talking," Mr. Wilson was saying, "we will listen to some of your critiques. *Stardust* is a difficult book for high school freshmen, and Mr. Purvis and I are anxious to see how some of you dealt with the book. Wendy, would you like to start us off?"

Wendy Rogers wasn't the smartest kid in the class, but she was the least self-conscious. She went to the front of the class without hesitation. Jake Wilson moved his chair over to the door to let her have his desk. Wendy smiled first at Mr. Wilson, smiled next at the class, and then maybe, Jerry couldn't be sure, smiled at Mr. Purvis.

"Paul Bernard is a great American writer," she began. "He wrote *Stardust* and many other famous books. Let me begin by telling you what *Stardust* is about."

Mr. Purvis closed his eyes and lowered his head. Jerry thought he could hear Jake groan. Wendy paid no attention. She rattled on about who was who in the retirement home. At the end of each paragraph she stopped and smiled at the class. When she came to the bottom of her third page, she smiled once more, said thank you, and returned to her seat.

Mr. Purvis opened his eyes and lifted his head. He nodded toward Jerry's copy of *Stardust*. "May I?" he whispered.

Forgetting about Paul's inscription, Jerry handed him the book. He wanted to see who was next on Mr. Wilson's hit list. It was George Klein, who wasn't any smarter than Wendy Rogers. Jerry felt pretty sure he would be the one after George to be called to the front of the room. He began to get angry. Mr. Wilson was playing games with him.

Out of the corner of his eye Jerry saw Mr. Purvis open the book. He read the inscription and made a silent whistle of astonishment. Then he reached out to pat Jerry on the leg and made a circle with the thumb and middle finger of his other hand. Jerry smiled a sick, weak smile. He *was* in for it.

George Klein wasn't much of a speaker. He started to stammer through his composition. It was clear George had not read the book. He kept looking at his friend Tim Mendoza and shrugging his shoulders. Tim was the brightest kid in the class. Any time you needed help, you called up Tim Mendoza. George had been talking to Tim, although it didn't appear to have done him much good.

Mr. Wilson kept glancing at his watch. When it reached ten-thirty, he interrupted George, who had just started on the last page. "Thank you, George. We're running out of time. We'd better let someone else have a turn." He fixed his gaze on Jerry. "How about you, Jerry? Will you honor us with your words of wisdom?" he said in a nasty voice.

As Jerry rose to his feet, Mr. Purvis held out the copy of *Stardust*. Jerry shook his head and walked slowly to the front of the room. Mr. Wilson moved from his chair by the door to a student desk right in front of Jerry.

Jerry squared his shoulders, widened his stance for support the way Mr. Bernard did, and unfolded his paper. He separated the first page. He realized he was timing himself to get through the ordeal. He figured if he read slowly, there wouldn't be too much time left for questions, and he might escape free and clear. Tomorrow, Mr. Purvis would talk, and after that, on Wednesday, he had music at ten o'clock. That left only Thursday and Friday to worry about when they came along.

He smoothed the first page out on Mr. Wilson's desk. "This is a pretty tough book to write about," he told the class, as if they didn't already know. He waited for the murmurs of agreement to die down. Mr. Wilson smiled and watched him, like a cat with a mouse in the corner.

Jerry read the first paragraph, pronouncing each word carefully. He could see Tim Mendoza doodling in his notebook. Wendy Rogers was smiling because she had caught on that Jerry's composition wasn't any better than hers.

He continued into the second paragraph. After the first sentence, Mr. Wilson leaned forward. "Who says it's his most important novel, Jerry? Where did you hear that?"

"I don't know. I must have read it, I guess." He remembered what it said on the back flap of the jacket. "It says so on the jacket. Could I have my book, please?" he called to Mr. Purvis.

The stranger held up the palm of his hand to Jerry, telling him to wait. He opened the novel to the back. "This is Paul Bernard's most important novel," he read. Then Mr. Purvis added a comment of his own. "That is what his publishers say. I agree with them, and with you, Jerry."

Jerry took a deep breath. Maybe it would be all right. He looked at his watch. Twenty minutes. He started to read again.

Mr. Wilson remained quiet until Jerry started in on telling the story. He cut in. "Are you going to tell us the plot for the rest of the paper, Jerry? We've already heard it twice."

Jerry pointed down to page three of his paper. "That's all I have, sir. Most of us have tried to tell you what the book is about, except maybe for Tim Mendoza. He probably has more to say about it." The class laughed, and Tim turned red.

"Except for you, Jerry Huffaker. You have much more to say than the rest of us, including Mr. Purvis. What has Mr. Paul Bernard confided to you about his greatest novel? Somewhere in that never-ending interview he must have told you how he came to write *Stardust* and what it means to him, the artist. It would be awfully strange if he hadn't." Mr. Wilson called to the back of the room. "Don't you agree, Will?"

Mr. Purvis didn't answer. He stared down at his lap again. He was embarrassed for Mr. Wilson, it was clear to Jerry. He could see that he was tormenting Jerry. The knowledge that he had a friend in Mr. Purvis gave Jerry strength. He shook his head. "No, he didn't tell me."

He had lied. That was a mistake, he understood at once. Lies were harder to defend than the truth. "Only about the hat," he said. "The hat the clown wears is like the hat Mr. Bernard's father wore all the time."

Mr. Purvis looked pleased and interested. Jake wasn't so interested in the hat. "What about the hat?" he demanded.

"The old brown hat the clown never takes off was Mr. Bernard's father's hat. That's all."

"Maybe he was bald," Jake said, and the class laughed. "What else did Mr. Bernard tell our star reporter? You haven't spent six months talking about an old brown hat every Saturday. What else did he tell you, Jerry boy?"

It was the "Jerry boy" that did it. He had had enough of being called "Jerry boy." "Nothing else I can tell you about,

Mr. Wilson," he said with as much dignity as he could muster, and returned to his seat. As he squeezed past Mr. Purvis, it seemed to Jerry he saw a faint nod of approval.

By the time Jerry was in his seat, Jake Wilson was striding toward him, his face contorted with rage. "By God, you'll tell me—I mean, us—right now, Jerry boy, or your name is six kinds of mud in this school. Why are you holding out on us? No more secrets. What do you think I brought Will Purvis here for? It's time to talk. Get back up to the front of the room. I didn't give you permission to go to your seat."

He reached down to drag Jerry from his desk. He took his arm and pulled. Jerry hunched down and held on to the desk. "I can't," he cried. "I can't do it. I won't do it. It's private."

"You'll do it or it will be the end of you." Jake Wilson pulled harder.

Jerry shook his head and hunched farther down into his desk.

The slap echoed around the room. It seemed to Jerry he heard the sound before he felt the awful pain in his ear and cheek. Tears of hurt and anger poured from his eyes. He stood up and drew back his fist.

Mr. Purvis, the fat little stranger, was on his feet before Jerry. He took the trembling Jake Wilson by the arm. "Come on, Jake, come with me," Jerry heard him say. The last he ever saw of Mr. Wilson was Will Purvis leading him out the door of the classroom.

That night, Dad didn't wait for Jerry to go to bed before he called Amy. As soon as he thought she was home from work, he was on the phone to Chicago. He used the kitchen phone right in front of Jerry, who was at the table cutting himself another piece of Dad's chocolate cake.

"It's all over town, Amy. Wilson has resigned. Not directly. He didn't have the courage for that. His friend called the principal's office and told them Jake had to take an extended leave of absence. Jake and his friend Purvis have gone to San Francisco."

Mom must have said something about bringing charges, because Dad said, "I don't think it would be a good idea. Jerry has been through enough. We've talked it over. I don't think he wants to be embarrassed any more."

Dad lowered his voice and carried the phone toward the dining room, but Jerry could hear him say, "That's not the real reason, Amy. He doesn't want to bring Paul Bernard into it. He won't have that. 'Paul has to get on with his writing,' he told me. 'We can't bother him now.'"

Mom said something else. Dad listened for a long time. At last, he said, "You have quite a boy here, Amy. But he needs his mom. Isn't it about time you headed for home?"

25

THE WIND WAS FROM THE LAND, WARM AGAINST THE BACKS
of Paul Bernard and Jerry Huffaker, who stood at the cliff.
Spring flowers were cropping up among the rocks. Along the
drive Jerry had collected a handful for Mrs. Bailey and
Lorna. He had pushed the bike with one hand in order to
hold the flowers in the other, taking care not to crush the
tiny wax petals.

"Another year," Bernard said, waving his arm crutch
around for no reason. He put it back down. "I don't know
why I didn't use these before," he told Jerry. "The gorilla
kept after me to use them, but I couldn't be bothered. I was
too used to my regular crutches. I felt safe with them. Now I
feel safer with these, can you imagine?"

There wasn't much Jerry could say to that. "Do you think
spring has come?" he asked. After spring came summer vacation.

"It's hard to tell along the coast. The wind can shift and it's winter again. But it's on its way. You can feel the softness in the air. You always knew back home when spring was on the way. Before I was born, Dad planted clumps of iris and daffodils down in the orchard. The orchard never amounted to much because Dad never got around to spraying the trees, and all we got were some scrabbly, wormy apples.

"The flowers spread like wildfire. By the time Mom died, the orchard was covered with daffodils first and then blue iris. When you saw the green spikes poking up through the dead grass, you could be certain spring was on the way. I used to cut armfuls of flowers and put them in a bucket to take up to Mom in the hospital. When the flowers were gone that spring, Mom was gone, too. Spring is a tough time for me. Lorna has trouble in the fall, she says. I have trouble in the spring."

The great man was quiet. He tested his crutches. It was harder to rock back and forth on them than on the others. He kicked a stone over the edge. It rattled down the slope and came to rest beside Harpo. He didn't move a whisker. Bernard laughed and shook his head.

"Mrs. Bailey says you had some trouble, too, Jerry. At your school."

"Not much," Jerry replied. He didn't want to talk about it. "Look! There's Mom going into the water first. You almost never see her go first. She likes to follow Harpo."

Paul looked down. "That's because she's a mother and has to protect herself. Harpo goes first to look out for sharks or whatever. Mrs. Bailey says that Wilson brute smashed you in the face. Is that right?"

"Yes, but it's not worth talking about. It's all over. It's in the past now."

"What's all over?" Lorna asked. She had come up from behind them with the mailbag. "Not much today," she told her father. "Only ten or twelve letters. You must be slipping. What's all over, Jerry? Not the marriage, I hope."

Jerry shook his head. It was Paul Bernard who answered Lorna. "That trouble with his teacher Mrs. Bailey told us about early in the week."

"Are you going to press charges, Jerry?" Lorna asked. "People like that shouldn't be allowed to go unpunished."

"It's all right," Jerry said. "He went away."

"You were looking after me, weren't you, Jerry?" Bernard said.

"A little bit, maybe. But it's all over now. My ear has gone down. I don't want to talk about it, please. It's all over."

Paul Bernard took a deep breath. And another. He spoke. "Things like that are never over. You can't put them aside and forget them." He nodded down toward his legs. "Look at those. More than thirty years ago my father blew them off with a shotgun. Do you think I can ever forget it's over, Jerry?"

Lorna gasped and drew back a step. Speechless with horror, she heard Jerry ask in a slow, calm voice. "Is that the accident, Paul?"

The great man spoke toward the horizon. "That's just a word I use. It wasn't an accident. Just like what Wilson did to you wasn't an accident. He probably couldn't help himself, but you couldn't say hitting you in the face was an accident."

"Was your dad drunk?" Jerry asked in the same calm tone. The last door to the secret was open. He had to keep it open. It wasn't so much that he wanted to know the dreadful secret for himself, but he had to hold the door open to let it escape. That was his job now.

"No drunker than usual, I suppose," Paul replied. "The drink didn't make him careless, just silent and, after a while, mean in his soul."

"He shot you on purpose. Why do you say that?" Jerry asked.

"I've kept asking myself that, right up to this moment. I tell myself he didn't want to lose me, which can mean he loved me in a crazy way and wanted me with him. Or he wanted to punish me, which means he hated me for leaving him. Either way I lost my legs."

Lorna, motionless in back of her father, sobbed softly. She wiped her face on the sleeve of her sweater. She looked at Jerry, pleading silently with him not to go on.

Jerry avoided her eyes. Now *he* had to know. "But you only left him to go to school. Kids have to go to school, even college. If you hadn't gone to college, you wouldn't have been a writer."

"Maybe, Jerry. Maybe not. The point is I went away from him because I wanted to. No one had to go to college where I grew up. Most of the kids didn't make it to high school. And I didn't go to be a writer. I went to escape my father. I had to go so I could breathe. He used his silence to suffocate me, to prove to me that he loved my mother. It was penance for neglecting her when she was alive, and I had to share it. I couldn't take it. I ran away to a little hick college and started to work my way through. When the war came I signed up the first week. Not for my country, but for myself. I imagine now that what I wanted was to get shot.

"Dad knew that. He laughed when I came home a couple of times and tried to explain it all to him. I tried to talk

· 151 ·

to him about other things, the farm, about my plans, about anything that would make him notice me. He'd push the old brown hat back on his head, go over to the kitchen cabinet to take a swallow from the bottle, and walk out of the room."

"You wrote the war book at the farm, you said," Jerry reminded him. "What did your dad think of that?"

"Nothing. He didn't know what I was doing. I wrote it because the paper was all I had to talk to at the kitchen table. I wrote that book right there at the table. I'd stop to fix Dad his lunch and supper and go on writing in the middle of all the dishes."

Lorna spoke for the first time. Her words held a rebuke for her father. "And you brought Meredith to that? You made my mother suffer that for a year?"

The great man turned to face his daughter. Crutches dangling from the arm clips, he reached out to seize her shoulders. "I had to. By then he really needed me. I thought he was losing his mind. I couldn't leave him. I'd seen a lot of killing in the war, soldiers dying with no one to help them. He was my dad and he needed me. I had to stay with him. Your mother understood that."

"Mom didn't tell me."

"Meredith was loyal, I'll say that for her. She was deep-down loyal. In the end I was the one who made us leave the farm, not Meredith. It wasn't that I couldn't take it. It was something different. I couldn't write and I had to write. We left.

"I used to go down to the farm to help with the carp and again in the spring to see the flowers and carry a basketful to Mom's grave. Dad never said hello or good-bye. The only thing left that made sense to me was Sam the Fish Man. He still drove the tank truck down to carry off the carp for the holidays. I tried to write a book about him once, but it didn't work. I think he meant too much to me by then.

"The last time I went down to help, Dad spoke to me. 'Let's go shoot some railbirds up in the marsh, Paul.'"

"He got the .410 and we poled the skiff up to the marsh. Even then there weren't many railbirds left. We took turns poling through the reeds. You had to pole from the front of the skiff in order to whack the grass with the pole to drive the birds into the air. I was poling and whacking. A couple of birds flew up, and Dad blew my legs off."

"It was an accident, Dad," Lorna cried. "It had to be an accident."

"It was no accident, Lorna. That's what I told myself for years, but it was no accident. Dad was the best shot in the county, drunk or sober. He wasn't going to hit someone in the legs from five feet away unless he wanted to. That's why he took the .410. A twelve gauge would have killed me.

"He tied what was left of my legs up so I wouldn't bleed to death and poled back to the truck and carried me up to the hospital. They had to take them off and that was that. As Jerry said, it was over and no need to talk about it anymore. I said to Dr. Manlove it was an accident and please not to tell anyone. He thought I was protecting Dad. He was wrong. I was protecting myself. Meredith came to take me back to the city, and there I stayed until I came here.

"The thing was I couldn't talk about it, especially after Dad died. It didn't make any sense to me, so I kept quiet."

"What did your dad die of?" Jerry asked. "The same thing as your mother?"

"The shotgun, Jerry, that's what he died of. He poled

the skiff up to the marsh about where the accident took place and shot himself. He was up there awhile before they found him. I went down to the farm and buried him next to Mom."

The great man took halting steps toward the great white house. Lorna held his arm. He put his arm around her shoulders. Jerry wondered who was helping whom. He wiped his eyes and went to where his bike was parked and fled down the hill.

26

WITH GROWING CONCERN, TED HUFFAKER LISTENED TO HIS
son's account of Paul Bernard's confession. Not only concern, but a troubled feeling of guilt. Jerry was confused and
upset. Ted had foreseen the direction Bernard's conversations with Jerry were taking, but he had never dreamed of
the horror of Bernard's "accident." He and Jerry had talked
it out; he had not intervened. And he had not intervened to
head off the dreadful confrontation with Jake Wilson. These
violent events coming so close together, and not so long
after Amy's departure for Chicago, could harm the boy for
the rest of his life. It was too heavy a load for an adolescent
to carry.

"Do you understand what Mr. Bernard was telling you,
Jerry?" Ted asked.

"It was pretty clear, Dad. There wasn't much I could say.
He believes his father shot him on purpose. I guess he told

himself it was an accident for a long time when he didn't really think it was. It must have messed up his life."

"Did it mess up his life or make him into a truly great writer, because he could understand other people's suffering and anger and disappointments?"

"Both. Paul hasn't had such a hot life without his legs, and he doesn't really care how great he is. Maybe he should have talked to a psychiatrist like you said he should."

Ted considered what he had once said in the light of what Jerry had told him now. It was his terrible secret that had driven Paul Bernard deep into his reflections about humanity and made him the famous author he had become. "I used to think that, Jerry, but now I'm not certain. Isn't it time for our ice cream?"

"Not tonight, Dad. I think I'll go to bed early." The Dairy Queen was part of the ceremony of the interview. Jerry already knew he could not bring himself to return to the big white house. He felt strange and uncertain. It was how he had felt the weeks after his mother left. Soon it would be summer vacation, he thought. And Mom might be coming home. He would try to think about the good things.

"Good-night, Son. How about going up to Point Lobos tomorrow to look at the seals? We can pack a lunch."

"I don't think so, Dad. I have some homework I have to do. Anyway, they're sea lions, not seals, most of them."

In the days that followed, Jerry kept his distance from his father. There were things he didn't want to talk about. He avoided being drawn into a discussion of them again. He stayed in his room, door closed, listening to his tapes and, to Ted's surprise, reading. He brought home several of Paul Bernard's books from the town library and was going through them, slowly, like his father. The bicycle rested, unused, in the garage. Ted said nothing. He waited—and talked with Amy.

"He's lonely, Ted," she said right away. "He's lost a friend—two friends, really. Bernard and Lorna. He feels betrayed. He had nothing to do with what happened a long time ago. He doesn't know what to do. He probably blames you a little bit, too. He's hoping Lorna will call, I think. Let him work it out his own way, Ted."

"Shall I call Lorna?" he asked.

"I don't think so. They must be having their own problems. Bernard is not a fool. He has to work things out, too. It would be hard for him to face Jerry after that disclosure. I'm sure he knows he shouldn't have laid his tragedy on Jerry. Bernard must feel that he's betrayed both his father and Jerry."

"It wasn't fair, Amy," Ted protested. "It was one thing to talk about himself to a kid to help get over his writing block. It was something else to dump that violence on him. It's like that crazy Jake Wilson."

"Things aren't always fair, Ted. It wasn't fair for me to walk out. It wasn't fair for you to keep me from working because you thought I should be like your mother. I could say now it's not fair for Jerry to avoid his father because he doesn't want to talk about something that hurt him. It's all part of growing up, Ted. Some of us do and some of us don't. It took Paul Bernard more than thirty years, or however long it's been, to become a man."

"And us, Amy," Ted asked. "What about us?"

"We're still working on it, Ted. I'll call you tomorrow if I have an answer. Take care, and don't push Jerry, please."

Amy's answer was simple, the announcement that she had bought a ticket on Flight 114, Chicago to San Francisco, arriving 3:20 Saturday afternoon. "All of me," she told Ted. "That includes two suitcases of dirty clothes and a heart full of hopes for the future."

Jerry said it was great news, but not much more. "What is she going to do?" he asked half suspiciously. It almost sounded as if Amy had become an outsider along with Ted.

"We'll have to work on that, won't we, Jerry?"

"I reckon," Jerry responded and picked up his book.

When the phone rang Friday evening, Ted answered it quickly. That Amy had changed her mind was his first fearful thought. But it wasn't Amy. It was Lorna Bernard.

"Hi," she said briskly in her Eastern accent. "How are you, Ted?"

There were things that Ted wanted to say. He let them pass. "We're fine, Lorna. How are you and your father?"

"We're okay. Dad and I were wondering if Jerry was coming up to visit tomorrow. We haven't seen him for the last couple of Saturdays."

Ted started to say that Amy was flying home tomorrow. He stopped. It was Jerry's business. "I'll get Jerry for you," he told Lorna.

Jerry turned his boombox down. "Lorna?" he asked in surprise. "Lorna wants to talk to me?" He didn't say, "That's great." It was obvious to Ted that he wanted to. "Thanks, Dad," he did say, and hastened without actually running to the kitchen phone. Ted went into his study and closed the door.

Jerry tapped on the door and stuck his head inside. "Lorna wants me to go up to the house tomorrow. Paul wants to continue with the interview, she says. I said I'd call back. What do you think, Dad?"

"I think you're old enough to decide for yourself."

"Mom's coming home for good? You're sure, about that, Dad?"

"We can't ever be sure about anything, Jerry, but I'd bet we'll make it this time. She plans to start a counseling service of her own."

"I'd sort of feel in the way at the airport," Jerry said. "It's between you and Mom. And, well, I don't know for sure, either, but I think they need me up there. I kind of ran away from them that afternoon and I never called to see what was going on. I feel bad about that."

"And you need Paul and Lorna a little bit, don't you, Jerry? They helped you through a rough time." He put his arm around his son to walk him to the phone. "I'll tell you what. You go up to the Bernards'. Afterward we'll take Mom to the Dairy Queen for supper. How about that?"

Jerry gave his father a hug. "It's a deal, Dad."

27

LORNA AND MRS. BAILEY WERE SEATED AT THE TABLE NEAR the kitchen, watching the great man with amusement. He was thumping around the kitchen like a big bear, using only one of his arm crutches.

"Come in, Jerry," he shouted. "Join the ladies at the table. I'll get you a root beer."

"He's cooking lunch for us, Jerry," Mrs. Bailey said. "I never thought I'd see the day. The crazy man has taken my job away from me."

"Mrs. Bailey is leaving, Jerry," Lorna confided. "Her daughter is having another baby, after all these years. Mrs. Bailey is going to look after it at home, so that Marsha can go on working."

Jerry understood now about Paul's taking charge of his fake legs and learning to cook. He wondered if Lorna was planning to leave, too. He hoped not. If she left, Mr. Bernard might take it into his head to leave, too.

"You can't trust women, Jerry," Bernard called from the stove. "As soon as Lorna came, Mrs. Bailey decided to leave. That's how they are."

"Dad," Lorna laughed. "I've been here seven years, even if you weren't aware of it most of the time."

"Don't listen to him, Lorna. I've been here over twenty-five and all I've heard him talk about is how well the gorilla looked after him. The fact is, Jerry, he never needed anybody at all."

"You want a two-egg omelette, Jerry, or three?" Paul asked. "With chili sauce inside or mushrooms and black olives, like Lorna's?"

"Two, with chili sauce, please." The three of them watched the great man lumber around the kitchen, holding their breath as he broke the eggs into the bowl with one hand.

"He learned fast, I'll say that for him," Mrs. Bailey remarked.

"Faster than I did, is that what you mean, Mrs. Bailey?" Lorna asked.

"Men are just better cooks, Lorna. We ought to accept that and move them all into the kitchen where they belong. There wouldn't be so much trouble in the world."

"My mother is coming into San Francisco this afternoon," Jerry announced. He hadn't been meaning to say anything, but it seemed the occasion for sharing news.

"That's wonderful, Jerry," Lorna exclaimed. "Did you hear that, Dad?"

The great man brought Jerry's plate to the table. "What are you doing here, Jerry?" he demanded.

"I thought about it. I decided it would be easier for Dad by himself. And I thought maybe you wanted to see me again."

"We did," Bernard admitted. "He's going to write, Lorna. No two ways about it. You wait and see. Jerry knows how people work. That's all you need to know, Jerry, how they work inside. Then you don't have to make it up." He paused. "Lorna and I will be here. You mustn't forget us when your mother is back. And now for the dessert."

From the cabinet Bernard took a three-layer cake with pink frosting. On top, he had sprinkled silver decorations and written in crooked blue letters, "Thank you."

"Hmph." Mrs. Bailey sniffed and put a tissue to her eyes. "You'll have to do better than that with your decorating, Paul. I hope it tastes better than it looks. I'll take a piece to Marsha anyway." She put her head down and let the tears flow.

When Mrs. Bailey had left in her rattly old Plymouth, Paul Bernard, Lorna, and Jerry sat on the deck. Bernard wore his sailfishing hat. "There's no point in going to the cliff, Jerry. Harpo and Mom have taken off up the coast. I'm sorry about that. Every three years or so they take it into their heads to visit their relatives or something. Come fall, they'll be back."

He looked to the horizon. The three were silent in the sunshine. "I'll be back in a minute," Lorna said. "Don't go away."

She returned with an old-fashioned, fake-leather book bag. She laid it in Jerry's lap.

"What's this?" he asked. He looked at Lorna, who was smiling, and Bernard, who was staring out to sea.

"Open it," Lorna said.

Jerry unbuckled the two straps. He opened the bag. It smelled moldy. Inside were hundreds of pages of crisp white typing paper.

He glanced at the great man. He had not moved. Jerry took out the first page. "Interview with a Bike Rider. Paul Bernard."

"It's the interview," Lorna said softly. "It's yours."

"Yours to keep," Bernard spoke at last. "There's a letter in the bag, too. I had my attorney draw it up. It's yours, free and clear. So is the bag. My father gave it to me for my birthday when I started writing my first book on the kitchen table at the farm. I used to use it for my manuscripts. I'd forgot about it somehow. Lorna rooted it out upstairs. Dad had written a birthday note on a piece of cheap lined paper. It was still inside the bag. I've read it again. It's made me think it was an accident after all. Whatever it was, it's over and done with."

"Dad gave me his picture," Lorna said, "the one from the filing cabinet that looks like you."

"Did you read this, Lorna?" Jerry pointed to his manuscript.

"I have a copy. I'll read it some day."

Jerry had a sudden thought. "What about the white pads and the box? What were you writing on the white pads, Paul? Lorna was afraid to look in the box."

Paul Bernard laughed. "I think she's peeped by now. Why don't you tell him, Lorna?"

"It's a novel, I guess. It's called *The Prodigal Daughter*. It seems to be about a girl who grew up without her father. Is that right, Dad?"

The great man did not respond. He was brooding again about the human condition. He had thrust his fake legs straight out in front of him and pulled Rick's cap brim down over his face. He reached out to take Lorna's hand. He held it tight.

28

———◆———

"THIS IS KIND OF THE LAST CHAPTER, I GUESS. HE CALLS IT 'The End of the Interview.'" Jerry looked at the last two pages of the interview. Paul had told him to read them if he really wanted to know.

Mom was sitting on the sofa in the living room next to Dad, close, the way Jerry had never seen her sit next to him. Dad had taken her hand and was holding it in his two hands. They had come back from the Dairy Queen, where Mom had said she still didn't think much of soft ice cream, but if it was part of the ceremony, she'd have some, only would they put a lot of chocolate sauce and nuts and whipped cream on top of hers, please.

"You mean," Mom said, "when you asked Mr. Bernard this afternoon what the birthday note in the book bag said, he told you to read the end of the manuscript he gave you? Why did he do that?"

"Because I asked, I suppose. I really wanted to know. He didn't tell Lorna or me what it said."

"But . . ." Mom said.

"Why don't you go on reading, Jerry?" Dad suggested. "We'll be quiet now." He lifted Mom's hand to his lips and kissed it softly. Jerry certainly hadn't seen that before, either.

"Okay," he said. "Here goes."

THE BOY: What did the note say that your dad put in the book bag?

THE WRITER: It said: 'This is from your mom and me. She would of got it for you. I don't know what you are doing at the table, but you can keep the sheets of paper in here. I hope it won't take you away from here. Because I love you.' When things got really bad with him, I used to read the note again, right up to the accident. Then I stopped and put the book bag away.

THE BOY: He said he loved you. I don't understand why he shot you.

THE WRITER: I went away. The boy became a man and left him. This wasn't what he wanted. He wanted the boy back, like he wanted my mom back. The man— his son—came back with a wife and a child-to-be. That wasn't what he wanted at all. He drove us away. He had lost the boy for good. Then, one time when I came to visit, he shot me. He wanted to keep me. That's what I used to think.

THE BOY: But you called it an accident. It had to be. He said he loved you.

THE WRITER: It didn't have to be. Maybe it was. Maybe it wasn't. Maybe it was love. Whichever, those are the things that run our lives, accidents and love. I think you understand that.

Jerry slipped the pages into his book bag.

"But," Amy persisted, "he wrote that before you even asked him about his father's note. How did he know?"

Jerry went and squeezed onto the sofa next to his mother. "Paul knew all right. He said, 'If you know people, you know everything you need to know.'"